The Hangman in the Mirror

Kate Cayley

Cover design by Sheryl Shapiro
Interior design by Monica Charny

Annick Press Ltd.

We acknowledge the support of the Canada Council for the Arts, the Ontario Arts Council,
and the Government of Canada through the Canada Book Fund (CBF) for our publishing
activities.

ONTARIO ARTS COUNCIL
CONSEIL DES ARTS DE L'ONTARIO

Cataloging in Publication

Cayley, Kate
 The hangman in the mirror / Kate Cayley.

ISBN 978-1-55451-357-4 (bound).—ISBN 978-1-55451-356-7 (pbk.)

 I. Title.

PS8605.A945H36 2011   jC813'.6   C2011-902667-8

Printed in Canada

MIX
Paper from
responsible sources
FSC® C003594

Published in the U.S.A. by
Annick Press (U.S.) Ltd.

Distributed in Canada by
Firefly Books Ltd.
66 Leek Crescent
Richmond Hill, ON
L4B 1H1

Distributed in the U.S.A. by
Firefly Books (U.S.) Inc.
P.O. Box 1338
Ellicott Station
Buffalo, NY 14205

Visit us at: www.annickpress.com

Cover images front and back: noose: ©Kelpfish; rust background: ©Genotar; leather
background: ©Justin Poliachik; additional rusty metal: ©Rachael Towne; front only: tarnish
on mirror: ©Brandy Sites; glass in mirror: ©Mytopshelf: all ©Dreamstime.com. Mirror
frame: ©art-4-art; cracks in mirror: ©scol22: both ©iStockphoto, Inc.

For Kiersten, Sarah, and Zach

Prologue

"Françoise Laurent, you are hereby sentenced to death by hanging, which sentence to be carried out in the month of December, in the city of Montreal, in the year of our Lord 1751. May God have mercy upon your soul."

The door, shut. The key, turning in the lock.

In prison, the world is smaller than I can imagine. There is nothing here. A bed of dirty straw, a bowl of stale water, a thin gray light moving across the floor of my cell. A young girl, myself, sixteen years of nerves and bones and blood, luck and will, determined breath and a still-beating heart.

They will hang me in the winter and I will hang dead in the snow. My face swollen, my spine broken, I will swing in the wind, in the wide open spaces of New France, and I will stand as a warning for all those who are born with nothing and wish for more.

A woman in my position, if there is no one else to marry, will marry Death.

What is it like to be married, I wonder?

Chapter One

"It's a mirror, Françoise."

"I know."

"To see your face in."

"I know."

"Fifteen years old. You're a lady now, a fine lady. Ladies must look to their faces."

"Yes, Papa."

"Happy birthday."

"Yes, Papa. Thank you."

It was a small mirror, in a tarnished and battered frame, and it was cracked along one side. I did not mention the crack. I knew the peddler my father had got it from, traded for the buttons off his soldier's jacket. Where the peddler had got such a precious thing, crack or no, I could not guess.

"It's beautiful, Papa."

"Yes, yes. Go along."

He smiled at me, his face creased with broken red veins. Then he kissed the top of my head, and turned away.

I went into the kitchen, where the laundry was bubbling over a pitiable fire. The smoke drifted out of the cracks in our dirty windows, stuffed with rags against the growing cold. Birthday or no birthday, we must meet the laundry orders or starve, as my mother often said to my father when he tipped out his remaining pay on the table, half drunk-up already.

The kitchen was an inferno of steam, the grease and sweat and soap of my mother's trade. Sheets and pillowcases, dresses and smocks and working shirts hung about the room like shrouds, from every chair and rack, from the rafters even, for where others hung food for winter, we hung other people's clothes. They bobbed in the rising warm air and they had, to me, a sad look. These clothes were mostly thin and drab, worn down with work and mending and the harsh lye soap of many washings. "I help those as cannot help themselves, poor stupid creatures," my mother liked to say, but it was nothing to be proud of. She took in the clothes of the slatternly, the poor, the bad housekeepers who could not sort themselves to do a proper spring washing after winter, or could not afford Madame Auclair, who ran a profitable business in the heart of the town. We took in the cast-offs of the cast-offs, I thought, to keep our bodies knitted to our souls.

"Fold those sheets for me, love," said my mother, half-turning in the light from the window. She was tall and thin as a broom handle, and the lump that was to be my brother (so they hoped, but I wished for a sister; I lit candles to the Virgin for it) made her look like she'd stuck a bolster under her dress.

"This is a precious order, my girl," she said, holding up a white shift to the light.

"Why, Mama?"

"Look at that, Françoise. That's good lace and good linen.

That's a fine lady's shift that she wears in bed with a fine husband. French lace and English woolens and beaver coats in that house."

She took my arm and made me feel along the soft length. It was a cloth like I'd never worn, and it felt smooth as water under my hands. Then she pointed to some faint brownish stains streaking down the skirt.

"But for all that, Françoise, that fine lady can't have a child. Stillbirth after stillbirth she's had. The maid brought me the bundle last night, in the dark so no one would see her and wonder why Madame needed her bloody linen washed clean all of a sudden. A boy, the maid told me. Her mistress should watch her maid's tongue. It does no good to hurry the linen away in the dark if the girl stands talking to the washerwoman, does it?"

She put the shift aside, lifted her iron from the fire, spat on it.

"Of course, there'd have to be some shame, for her to send her washing to us. I won't tell you her name, having some sense, for your tongue's worse than the maid's, but she's the wife of a rich trader, my girl, with a warehouse full of furs to ship to France. Such women do not send their washing to be done in two-room huts like ours, Françoise."

I nodded.

"Still, if I can't get the blood out, it does us no good."

She turned away, her shoulders hunched, swaying a little on her feet.

"Step lively, Françoise, and fold those sheets, like I asked. Don't stand there dreaming or I'll pull your ears."

I stood my ground, shifting from foot to foot.

"Mama?"

"What? What now?"

"Mama, I must go into market."

"Do you think I am rich, to have you spend all I make on sweets?"

"Mama, there is nothing to eat in the house. Not a scrap."

She turned round again.

"Don't fear, we will set in stores for winter. Louis and Mathilde will help, as they always do."

"I am sure they will, Mama, and the more fools they, to help us always and get nothing back. But whether or not they help us then, I must eat now."

"You eat too much."

She clutched my shoulder, which was sharp and bony. I shrugged her off. Sighing, she took down the box where she kept the coins, and shook it out on the table. Nothing fell out but an old cork and two dead spiders.

"Well, well. See. There's nothing to do."

She put it back on the shelf.

"If you must, take your cloak and go. Find Giles the baker and get him to give you the stale loaves on credit. He'll do it for me, for the sake of the old days. He owes me. Tell him that."

I winced, but her back was to me again. I knew what "owing" meant. Besides, the thought of another meal of stale crusts made me gag.

"Tell him we'll pay him when this laundry order is settled. Monday. Tuesday at the most. Or ... or Wednesday, maybe."

Then, perhaps remembering what day it was, she stroked my face. Her breath was sour, but her voice was steady still. I could see the open bottle standing on the windowsill, though it was not yet noon. She ate little, even with the baby. Those who drink like fishes seem to not want much food, but I, not being so afflicted, was hungry as a wolf.

"Françoise?"

"Yes, Mama."

"It's clothes, my girl, fine clothes, that make some women ladies and others servants and washerwomen. Nothing else. I scorn such women, I spit upon them."

And to show me, she spat again, this time on the floor in a ragged circle at my feet. I put on my patched cloak and went.

As soon as I was out of sight of our house, I pulled out the mirror and looked into it. My face stared back at me, thin and narrow, tallow-sallow, my teeth all jostling for room in my small pale mouth, my eyes so black you cannot see my pupils, as my mother would say, and my hair falling thin and tangled and dark. I was no great beauty, but I was pleased with myself all the same. And now I had a mirror to show me my face anytime I liked.

The road I was walking wound through trees, with houses here and there, slanted shacks like ours that let in every breath of air. We lived on the outskirts of the town, outside the fortified walls. Beyond us was darkness, woods, rocks, water—the end of the civilized New France. We were all afraid of the wild that lay at our backs, though in truth, it was still houses and roads for a while yet, before any real wilds began. Don't go far from the house except to get into town, my mother said. Always look over your shoulder, always say a prayer when you walk alone at night. The wilds are full of ghosts and monsters. I shivered.

But now it was bright day, and no monsters were to be seen. Even so, I picked my way carefully, for the road was full of sinking mud. Though it was coming on winter, my feet were still bare, tough as my boots, which I did not often wear. Why get them dirty when feet stain far less easily, and are simpler to mend when torn by stone, glass, or wagon wheels? I was proud of my hard feet, my hard fists, my hard voice.

I walked more quickly as I got into town, hoping to get to market in good time to see the kitchen maids from the grand houses, carrying their baskets full of food. I stayed well away from the soldiers, parading like roosters about the streets or stumbling in and out of the taverns, where they would sit all day playing cards when they were not on duty, and sometimes even then. A few of the men who knew my father shouted out tipsy greetings, and two recruits catcalled after me, as they would after anything that had the shape of a girl, but I passed on.

I threaded my way from street to street, admiring the sturdy fastness of the great houses, where the fur traders lived. Someday, I would live in a merchant's house, I thought, and be a lady, if all that divided us was fine clothes.

"Oh, the pleasure of love is fleeting, But the sorrow of love lasts."

I turned my head and saw a red-haired boy singing to himself, tagging behind his father, who was pushing a barrow full of things to sell at the market. I hurried on, scurrying like a mouse full tilt round the hairpin corners and back alleys, past the disapproving stares of those most holy and pinched ladies, the Grey Nuns, out for their prayerful walks, their habits flapping all about. I stuck my tongue out at them as I passed.

The market hummed and bustled this time of day. Great cuts of meat swung on cruel hooks, the bloody red mottled with the creamy white of fat and sinew. The stalls, even this late in the season, were rich with the hardier green things and all the different reds and yellows of apples. Some stalls even had more delicate plants, lettuces and the like, grown carefully under glass and hoarded like gold against the coming winter full of old potatoes and carrots. Those who had money to buy would. My stomach complained as I looked about me. The smell of the fish, fresh and salted, laid out on the slabs with dead eyes staring at the sky, made my mouth water. But I made my way to the baker Giles, with his stall of puffed greasy loaves. He was a wizened sly little man with a twice-broken nose, oddly bulging arms, strong from heaving sacks of flour, and a shuffling walk. I doubted that he felt he owed my mother, and I was not about to tell him so. He scowled as I approached.

"More bread? More? I've not been paid for three weeks, and every week you tell me 'soon.' But it never comes. There's no more for you."

"But—"

"No good, no good. No money, no more."

I gritted my teeth, then smiled, tugging at a twist of hair. "It's my birthday though. Today. Fifteen years old, a lady. Please."

He snorted, a sharp quick grunt like a pig.

"Not you, my girl, you'll never be a lady. Father's a drunken soldier who can't keep a pot to piss in, and as for your mother ..."

He let that hang in the air, leering at me, and I made my eyes fill with tears, which was a good trick I knew. His battered face softened, and he smiled, showing his four good teeth.

"Now, now. There now. I speak hard, Françoise, I speak hard. The cold coming on makes me sharp."

I let the tears fall, wiped my cheek with the dirtier hand so that a smudge of earth would smear gray across it.

"Don't take on. Here, I'll get you the bread."

From a basket under the table he took out an old loaf, the crust all cracked and broken.

"Let it be two," I said, making my voice wobble. Pushing my luck.

He frowned, thinking me forward, then slowly drew out a second loaf. This had the beginnings of a coat of mold growing over it. But I could scrape that off, no trouble.

"And now, get away with you, Françoise. But Monday it must be, tell your mother. Monday it must be when her washing orders are settled, for poor old Antoine Laurent never keeps his pay long enough to quit his own debts. Here. Take it and go."

I curtsied, dried my eyes.

"God's blood, it's not your fault to have such parents. Some do well in this land, and some do not," he said complacently, though why he thought a rickety bread stall was a great good fortune compared to mine, I could not see. But I thanked him, all the same.

Despite the loaves tucked into the ripped lining of my cloak, despite the mirror in my skirt pocket, I felt like the mud under his feet to have cried so, and I walked away imagining myself swooping out of a carriage and swirling clouds of musk perfume into his face as I averted my eyes from someone so unworthy of my notice. How that was to be, I did not know. I was filthy, a mess of bruises, darning, sluttish fallen hems, underwear like cat piss. I had to scrape and smile to stingy bakers. Some do well in this land, and some do not.

And then I saw the barrow, and the red-haired boy with his father. He was not really a boy, older than I was surely, and grown to full height, but his wrists stuck out thinly from his jacket sleeves, and his hair was soft and his eyes a little dazed, his skin freckled and gray-white as a skinned fish. An easy mark. Behind him, he'd carelessly left a sack untied, and vegetables had fallen onto the cobbles—a cabbage and four potatoes. I counted quickly, pretending to look elsewhere. They were on the ground already, half-rolled away. Helping yourself to what falls to the ground is not stealing; it's just taking what fortune offers. I thought of a soup, thick and hot. I thought of the stale bread, softened by dipping, and of licking the bowl clean at the end. I would make a good soup, and we would eat well tonight.

I snuck my way round the edges of the square until I was behind the father and son. I eyed their wares, calculated their attentions. I wished I were brave enough to attempt a chicken from the row of pale plucked birds lining the front of the table. As I watched, a woman approached, her heels clicking on the stones. She had handsome shoes, being the shoemaker's wife. She leaned over the table, inspecting the poultry, clucking in her throat as if she were a chicken herself.

"Madame."

The man was all smiles, and the son stood suddenly straighter, his heels together, a copy of his obsequious father.

"I should like to order a dozen birds, or perhaps twenty in all, if you have them." Her voice was nasal and pinched.

My eyes widened with the thought of ordering a dozen birds, or more, like it was nothing.

"I will put them in stone jars with lard for the winter."

"Very wise, Madame. Will you take some now, and the rest I shall deliver? I have the birds, as you see."

As she picked and chose, fussy and slow, I saw my chance.

Dropping to my knees, I waddled forward, bundled the cabbage and potatoes under my skirt, and was off down the side alley, headed roundabout ways toward home with my skirt all bulged out in front of me.

"Hey! Stop! Stop! Thief!"

The boy had seen me. I broke into a run and heard him pelting after me, slipping on the fishy stones.

On my own, I was as fast as an eel heading downstream, but I was so bent over with the awkward load that it slowed my pace. I ducked from street to street, turning corners, doubling back, hoping to lose him, but just as I had hid myself in a doorway, thinking he would pass, my luck gave out. I could hear his footsteps, hesitant, growing nearer, then pausing. I held my breath. I knew that pause; he was unsure, another moment and he would turn and go away, beaten. But just then the door I was flattened against opened and a fat woman bulked her way out, scolding.

"Out! Out! Out of here!"

I crouched down, held onto her skirt.

"Madame, you must save me from this villain! He means me harm!"

"She's a thief," said the boy, coming up and standing over me.

"I'm not!"

"If you don't believe me, look under her dress."

"I don't care, either of you," said the woman, wearily. "Just get out from my doorway."

And she chivied me off her doorstep and shut the door, leaving us standing there in the narrow street, facing each other.

"Thief. Give them back."

"Make me."

He stared, then smiled with a lordly air.

"Don't be silly. You're only a girl. Just give them back and I will say no more about it."

I stepped back. He stepped forward. One more step and I could make the alley and be gone.

"Give them back."

I did not answer. Then he sprang.

I think he only meant to frighten me, believing me perhaps a timid thing who would drop the load and be off, leaving him to carry his spoils back to his proud father. I did drop them, but only to gain the use of my arms and legs. I knocked him back on his feet, clawing at him, and we both fell, rolling and rolling on the stones. I felt the sharp edge of a doorstep cut me above the eye and I heard ripping cloth. He cursed me foully, for I'd torn his shirt and I was glad—it had been so fine, and he could not do much damage to my rags. I got two good handfuls of his hair and pulled, and he kicked me between the legs and I kicked back the same, which had better effect for he squealed and threw me off and drew away.

I was sorry then, and I came near, hoping to offer him my open palms and show the fight was done, but he hit me hard in the shoulder, spinning me round. Catching my breath, I bit him. I caught him on the fingers of his right hand and held hard until I tasted blood, metal-salty and warm, and then I drew back, spitting.

"Enough?"

"Thief! Thief!"

"I'm sorry. I did not mean to bite so deep."

I offered my handkerchief. He snatched it and wrapped it round his hand, never minding the dirt. I waited, not knowing what would happen next, but he stood still before me, angrily weeping and cursing, and I grew impatient.

"Fair trade, then," I said, picking up the vegetables and my two loaves, which luckily were so hard that they'd held their shape.

"Fair?"

"My rag for your rotten vegetables. Fair trade."

He did not move.

"You should not cry so."

"You bit me."

"A nip, a nothing. There won't even be a scar."

I hovered, still clutching my bundle.

"Go away. Go away. Go on."

He kicked a stone at his feet, and I saw he could not bear for me to see how I had shamed him. I turned and walked away, the vegetables cradled in my apron, and knew he watched me until I turned the corner and was gone from his sight.

When I reached my own door, I found my father had already left. My mother, singing and less steady on her feet, was still busy with the orders, and the room was thick and bleary with the steam and the smell of drink. Without a word, I gently laid the bread on the table. Then, under her astonished eyes, I shook my skirt out, took out the chopping board and the knife, and began, happily, to cut.

Chapter Two

I paid for the bread on Tuesday, first thing in the morning. My parents, bleary with drink, had already spent half the money brought in from that fine lady's bloody shift before I managed to haggle out of them the price of the loaves so I would not be shamed before the baker. "Some do well in this new land, and some do not," he told me again as he counted the coins, smirking at my discomfort. I had to sneak my way from stall to stall, fearful of coming face to face with the red-haired boy or his father. Yet when I did catch sight of the boy, I could not help staring at him, squinting to see if there was any bandage on his bitten hand, or any lasting mark. From what I could see (peering carefully from behind a woman's skirts), there was nothing at all, and I dismissed him in my heart as a whining coward.

When I got home, I found my mother sleeping in her chair, the wash water nearly boiled away and the day's orders not even properly begun. Her head lolled against her chest and she snored gently. I thought of kicking her awake or leaving her there and going off by myself to see what I could scrounge to eat, but her sleeping sighs and flushed face moved me to pity. I took the pot off the fire and drew more water, not putting it on to boil again but letting it stand until

I was ready to wake her. I took stock of the stains, and of which clothes belonged to which customers, and rolled up my sleeves, looking ruefully at my chapped and reddened hands. I hated the smell of soap, rancid from the rendered lye, rough from the ashes. For as long as I could remember, I had hated it, hated the labor of saving the lard to make it, buried in the earth all year, hated the smell of it boiling and bubbling in the soap cauldron each spring. It was foul, and made our skins crack and bleed. But if I could not be a lady, at least I could be a washerwoman, and save us from starving altogether.

I knew it was not right that a child should pity her parents, but mine were pitiful. They were quarrelsome, drunken, full of debts and troubles, and I had to pity them if I was to rise above their lot. Their lot was very low, as I had heard them say often enough, their voices thin with complaint. My father had come from France a hopeful soldier for the swelling ranks of the army, and had found it a ragtag and makeshift outfit, where men fought over trifles and played endless games of cards because they were bored, hungry, alone. My father got a liking for cards, which helped the liking for drink that he'd already had, and soon his pay was owed to others before he earned it. He told me he thought he would go mad from loneliness, and would have taken any whore that would have him, and, laughing till he coughed, he added, "And that's just what I did, for look at your mother," and she cursed him and boxed his ears, which made the laughing turn to coughing in earnest, and then cursing of his own.

It was not a kind thing to say, but it was a true one. My mother had been a Paris whore, but she'd wanted something better. She heard tales of the wonderful land of New France, and how it was full of men wanting wives. So, sick of old France and full of a spirit of adventure, off she went. At least that was the story she told me. But as I got older I wondered if she'd been put on the ship by force, as a disgraceful creature that Paris wanted to be rid of. Either way, the journey was long, and she wished for home by the time the last of land had slipped from sight. But there was no help for it; she was bound for Quebec.

She said when she staggered out of that boat that had been little better than a floating coffin and saw the hard cold town that seemed carved out of the rock, she thought she'd arrived in hell. I think, in her simplicity, her hazy sense of things, she'd expected the pier to be lined with men, all waiting for a good strong wife, like when the Bride Ships had sailed from France a generation before. But there was of course no one to meet her, and winter was coming. So, not knowing what else to do, she knocked on the fortified wooden doors of the Ursuline convent and wept to the nuns that she was a poor penitent woman, come to earn her bread and learn goodness at last. Seeing how desperate she was, they put her to work in the laundry and called her "the wretched one" and told her Christ had died for her sins.

And slowly she learned the ways of the town and heard

also the stories of Montreal. How it was full of soldiers and fur traders and merchants shipping their furs to France, how there were taverns and dancing, how the men staggered home with all their money gone, how bad women plied their trade along those stone streets. And she began to dream that she would go there, and with the spring she went, paying for the journey with the very last of her hard-earned coin. And what did she find? A wilder, rougher town, full of unhappy soldiers and cruel-eyed men of business and the voyageurs crazed from long months in the woods. But at least the taverns were warm, and she was sharp and quick. And so she met my father, a broken soldier, his cuffs frayed and half his buttons gone. He staggered into her one night in an alley, and she thought he seemed as good as any she could get, which was most likely true. So they were married.

He gambled and drank, and she drank too. She set up a trade in washing, helped at first with the only other trade she knew. She went along this way until she got too worn and sickly for the men to care for her much, which was just as well. My father would have keeled over where he stood, if he'd known, and he could not be blind forever. But all in all, they grew used to one another, and that was a kind of love.

They told me things they did not tell each other. That was just the way things were in our falling-down house. I was the only child they had to tell things to, though my mother had borne ten. I was the last. The rest passed out of the world before I'd even learned to walk, and I learned early. And now, all their hopes were centered on the child she carried. "A boy," my father would say, staring hard at her round belly. "It must be a boy, do you hear? Clever and strong." And my mother would nod, her hands clutched around her bulk.

As I heaved the sheets, my mother stirred and moaned in the chair. I went and touched her shoulder, and she kicked a little in her sleep. I was about to wake her when I heard a tap on the window.

"Françoise, come outside."

Squinting through the glass, I saw Marie and Isabelle, their white faces peering up over the sill.

"What is it?" I whispered, fearing to wake Mama.

"A hanging! There's to be a hanging today! Our brother said so!"

"When?"

"Now! Will your mother let you come?"

I grinned.

"My mother is asleep, God help her. If I don't wake her, she'll be none the wiser."

"Come then."

Seeing the excitement in Marie's face, I sighed and looked at the piles of washing. These two sisters were the only companions I had, really. They came from nearly as disreputable a household as my own. They were as ragged as I, and I liked them for it. Marie was my age, Isabelle a little younger, both pale as white mice. I looked again at the washing. Yet it would be something, to see a hanging. We had so few, and I had never seen one. I tiptoed past my mother, grabbed my cloak, and off we went, chattering all the way.

"My brother says they turn black when they're hanged."

"He says that's after they've been left a bit, stupid, not all at once."

"How do you know, Isabelle, you never listen anyway."

"What I heard," I put in hastily, for the sisters fought like cats and I did not want my outing spoiled, "is that the condemned man must try to jump up as high as he can. That way his neck will break quickly. Otherwise the hangman ties his hands and pushes him off, which makes it take a long time. A hangman's knot is terrible. The more you struggle, the more the rope pulls taut. You choke to death slow. If your neck breaks, it doesn't hurt."

"How do they know it doesn't hurt?" Isabelle asked in a fearful whisper.

I had no answer, and we walked on in silence, thinking about the drop the condemned man must face.

When we got to the square, it was crowded with people. Men, women, children—all had turned out to see the spectacle. Faces were whipped red from the cold wind that blew off the water. Neighbors cried greetings to each other, and an old woman sold trays of steaming meat pies while a peddler called out that he had a pack-full of ballads for sale, describing the fearsome crime and the terrible death of the criminal, which seemed nonsensical to me, as he was not dead yet.

"What did he do?" I heard Isabelle say. None of us knew.

"Probably stole the silver plate from some merchant's house," Marie said wisely.

"Why that?" I asked.

She shrugged.

"Isn't that something they hang people for?"

"I can't *see* anything!" Isabelle whined, her lip trembling. She was twelve, but could still be a baby when she wished. We pressed as close as we could in the thick crowd. We jostled forward, but were kept out by hostile elbows. I tried to squirm my way through, and a man kicked me in the shins.

"Stay back. This is my place, stay in the back."

I grumbled, but did not try to press in again.

Then a great roar went up. A man was being led to the scaffold. The executioner was behind him, and behind the executioner walked an old priest, his robes billowing about him in the wind. Seeking a better vantage, I dragged Marie and Isabelle out behind the crowd.

"Let me stand on your shoulders and shimmy up this signpost. Then I can call down what I see."

"Why should only you get to see?" Marie asked, her hands on her hips, her chin stuck out.

"Well … well … let me go first and then we'll take turns."

The signpost was tall, wrought iron, and full of twisting bars my hands might cling to if I could manage to avoid the wooden sign that swung crazily in the wind. They hoisted me as best they could, and at last I scrambled up, standing unevenly on their shoulders.

I could see clear across the crowd now, though I was too far away to hear anything. The scaffold was dark against the gray buildings, and hazy in the brilliant fall sunlight. Yellow leaves scudded before it in the wind. The priest kept his head down, shutting his eyes tight, his lips moving. I wondered if he was praying, and thought perhaps he meant us to think so, when in truth he was only shutting his eyes against the fierce wind. His scant gray hairs were whipped all around his balding head, and he looked a fool. I wondered if my thoughts were heresy, and wanted to cross myself just in case, but I was afraid I might fall if I loosed my hold.

I was disappointed by the sight of the condemned man, who was standing by the priest. He seemed so ordinary, if a little unkempt with his dark hair stiffened like straw around his white face, and a wild beard. I had expected to see a madman, some monster from my nightmares, chomping his teeth at the crowd and hurling oaths with his final breath. He held himself very still, his eyes staring wide and empty. His lips moved, a quick mumble. I wondered if perhaps he was simple in the head. Then I realized, watching his mouth, that he really was praying, more sincerely than any prayer I had ever seen, and that he held his body still and his eyes wide from the purest, most terrible fear. I felt myself drawn into a pit as I looked at his moving lips, his gasping breath. He glanced now and again at the wooden frame of the scaffold and the rough coil of rope that hung from it. Then his knees seemed to buckle, and he clutched the arm of the priest, who looked astonished and almost angry, but who supported him as best he could so that they swayed together like two drunk men stumbling down an alley in the dark.

"My *turn*," Marie hissed at me. I didn't answer. I kept my eyes fixed on the man.

"Let me up. I can't see a thing. Let me up!"

"No!"

"It's my *turn*."

"Not yet!"

She pulled at my skirt, trying to drag me down. I kicked her shoulder and she stepped back, making me lose my balance. Isabelle, not knowing what to do, stayed where she was, swaying under my weight. Marie stood out of reach, her arms folded.

"Help me!"

She shook her head. I steadied myself and was about to climb down and let her get on my shoulders when a great cry went up from the crowd. I was so startled by the noise that my foot slipped from Isabelle's shoulder, but instead of falling to the ground I wrapped my legs tight around the post and ducked my head out of the way of the swinging sign. Somehow I did not fall, but I could not get up or down. Isabelle moved back beside her sister, both on tiptoe, trying to see.

I saw plainly. The hangman had stepped to the front of the platform and now held up his arms. The crowd howled, a strange sound that was half rage and half celebration. Not sure what to do, I made a few feeble sounds; I could not find the heart for more. Suddenly, everyone around me seemed like beasts, and I wished only to go home, but could not get myself down. There were more people now, people huddled all around below me, and I could not see my way out.

The hangman was also ordinary, dressed in a commonplace working shirt, a threadbare coat, and stained breeches. He moved slowly, almost lumbering, for he was a big, heavyset man who seemed to labor under his own weight. Or perhaps he knew the people wished for a show, and had no wish to cheat them, though they jeered him as much as they cheered. He took the condemned man by the arm and guided him toward the bench that stood under the swinging rope. They stood beside it, and he tied the man's hands behind his back and looped the rope about his neck. Then the priest came and stood by the man, and a clerk read out the sentence, but with the wind and the noise of the people, I could not hear much. I heard, as if an echo, the words "forgiveness" and "peace" and then "until you are dead," and the day of the year it was, and something about France and the king.

The hangman hoisted the man roughly onto the stool and held his legs hard, waiting for the right moment to pull the stool away and begin the long, choking death.

Jump, I thought to myself, begging the man in my mind. Jump. Just jump. Let it be quick. Let it not hurt.

The man stood still, though his lips moved. On the stool, he was tall enough for all to see him now. Below me, I could hear Marie's and Isabelle's squeals.

Suddenly, the condemned man kicked free of the grip on his legs, kicked backward, and caught the hangman full in the face, and he fell back, yelling, his hands held to his nose, which spouted blood. In that moment, as the priest stared with an open mouth, as the clerk and the soldiers ran forward, the man jumped. A high, high jump, like a fish leaping from the water in springtime. He jumped clear of the stool, his staring eyes flashed in the sun, he fell, and the rope snapped his neck. The crowd groaned in disappointment, cheated of the kill. But I had watched the man's face as he leaped, and saw in him such determination, such will, that I wanted to laugh for joy. He had done it.

The man swung limp. One leg twitched and was still. It was over.

☗ ☗ ☗

When I got back home, my mother was still asleep in the chair. All around her were the mountains of clothes: the clean and folded piles I had finished and sorted, and then the grubby heaps, still waiting for the water. The fire was nearly out. I had been gone longer than I'd meant to be. The afternoon light spread low through the windows.

"Mama," I said, speaking softly.

She opened her eyes and stared at me blankly. I could see by her face that for a moment she did not know where she was.

"Ah, I must have nodded off there."

"Mama, I will set the water going again. You must get up now."

"Must!" she yelled, staggering from the chair. "Don't say must, my girl, or I'll give you a clout!"

I moved away, and she went to pick up the washboard, and saw all I had done. She turned, her eyes gentle.

"Françoise. You're a good girl, to help me so, a good girl."

Her voice was slurred.

"It's nothing, Mama," I said, turning from her and plunging my hands in among the biggest sheets. "It's nothing, no trouble."

"A good girl."

She swayed, clutched the edge of the windowsill. I would rather she was sharp than this.

"Stop it, Mama. You must pull yourself together some way. These are all late. We will get them done by tomorrow night if we work very hard. Come on."

And she straightened up, her eyes a little clearer.

"Yes, yes, you're right. I'm better now."

Shaking her head like a cat, she saw I had my cloak on.

"Well, where have you been, then?"

I did not answer, and began to stoke the fire, blowing on it carefully as I fed it.

"Trying to beg ribbons from the peddler? Or stealing vegetables? You'll hang yet, my girl, mark my words."

This was better; this was her old self, her tone half-whining, half-joking.

"I was at a hanging. The man jumped and broke his own neck, so everyone came away disappointed."

Her eyes were brighter then.

"I remember the hangings in Paris!" she sighed. "They were much grander than here. People hung out colored flags, and everything you could possibly want was for sale. It's a poor show here; I haven't been to one in years. Nothing much to it."

"There were some lovely meat pies and a ballad on the condemned man," I said, trying to make it sound like something.

"I thought as much. Why, in France there would be pastries and whole pigs and chickens roasting on the spit, right there in the square. The bakers would work all night to have fresh things to sell, and there would be such a crush of people, and all eager and hungry. And the peddlers would come from all over the city, from further off even, if word spread. With ribbons and brooches and all sorts of trinkets. A gentleman I knew bought me a brooch once—"

"Yes, Mama, a pewter rose. I know."

"It is in my trunk, and you will have it after I am dead. Poor motherless girl."

Her eyes filled with drunken tears at the thought.

"Well, well, tell me more about the hangings, then," I said hastily.

"Ballads and books and all kinds of things for sale, too, for those who could read—all arranged in wooden stalls, with pictures, all true, and all very sad. Once I saw a count executed for his crimes, I don't remember what he did, a murder or some such thing, and he had written a book in prison, all about the terrible things he had done, and they sold it right there beside the scaffold. It sold well. He died smiling."

"Yes, Mama."

In my head I still saw the face of the man as he jumped.

"And the priests would preach sermons to the crowds, and the criminal would be paraded through the streets and the priest would roar, 'Do you repent? Do you renounce the devil and all his works?' And if the man said yes, the crowd would clap and cheer. It was a fine, fine sight."

She laughed, remembering. I laughed a little too, to keep her company.

"And sometimes, if the man was very bad, there would be torture, and then we were all quiet with the awe of it and the man would cry out, 'O God, help me,' and it was a most sobering thing."

She took a swig from the bottle.

"Don't look at me so, Françoise, I am only a little thirsty. Anyone would think you were a nun, and no child of mine neither."

She stared off reflectively above my head. I bustled round her, determined to get something done before dark.

"Ah, the business I would do, on hanging days in France, the great mass of people. Not like here. Nothing much to it here. Just wheel them out and push them off. Isn't that so?"

"Mama," I said briskly, "whether or not it is so, we must make haste. So roll up your sleeves and help me."

And we fell to work.

Chapter Three

We didn't meet the orders on time. That night, my father shook me awake.

"Françoise. Wake up. The baby's coming. Run for the midwife."

His eyes were huge. He was as frightened as a trapped rabbit. We both knew it was too soon.

I hurtled along the dark paths, not toward the town but away along the darker paths. The midwife, Mathilde, lived not far, but I was so frantic in my haste that I stumbled and fell several times, the branches of trees tearing at my face and my skirts. I beat them back blindly, thinking only of my sister, who was to be born that night too small and frail for the big world.

"Let me in! Let me in! It's coming too soon!" I shrieked, hammering on Mathilde's crooked door. Her husband, Louis, opened it and I almost fell against him. He stood there looking foolish in his nightshirt and cap, his eyes heavy with sleep.

"Mathilde! I must see Mathilde."

He steadied me, his hands on my shoulders, calling behind him, "Come, wake up, it's the Laurent girl and her mother's come on too soon." Then, turning back to me, he drew me quickly into the house.

I waited, jigging from foot to foot in impatience, as Mathilde dressed in the bedroom and Louis helped her to pack her bag. Their house was two big rooms of stone, made from years of great labor. The walls were four feet thick, stuffed with ashes and sawdust, and proof against the cold, with low, small windows shut fast now against the dark. Compared to our shack, the house seemed large as a cathedral. The room was dim and smoky from the low fire, and smelled of blood and leather, for Louis made his living stretching and drying skins for one of the Montreal warehouses that would then send them on to France. The firelight played fearsomely over the hides that hung all about. Some still had attached the face of a mink, a fox, a beaver—the muzzle open, the nose gone, the eyes hollow holes. I ran my hands over a silver fur, which still held the oily warmth of the living creature, and calmed myself by imagining the coat it would make, the people who might wear it back in France, where I would never go.

"Come, Françoise, come with me," said Mathilde in her low rasping voice. She took my hand as though I were a small child, not nearly grown, and we went out.

I wanted to run, thinking of my mother's pain and my father's fear, but Mathilde walked, swiftly and solidly, still holding tight to my hand. The night was bright with stars and a full moon. When we got inside the house, I could hear my mother, breathing low, groaning through a set jaw, and I saw my father feebly trying to build up the fire. Mathilde chivied both him and me into the kitchen and shut the bedroom door, telling me she would call for me if she needed an extra pair of hands. My father sat down by the washbasin and sank his head onto his folded arms, and I, not knowing what else to do, took to sorting the washed and unwashed sheets into proper piles. So when Mathilde came and told us that the baby, my brother, had come and gone from us, living only long enough to gasp a puny, unready breath, she found my father fallen into a light sleep, and me sitting listless in the middle of the floor, surrounded by dirty sheets.

She led us into our bedroom, where my mother was half-lying in my parents' bed, holding in her arms the smallest baby boy I had ever seen or imagined. His head was large, and his face scrunched forward in the front of it, and the skin of his thin body was so stretched and waxen that I could see through it to the red and blue of his veins. He was strange, and beautiful. My father turned and went out of the room again, and I knew, looking at him standing just outside the doorway with his back to us, his shoulders hunched up round his ears, that he was trying not to weep. I wanted to go and help him, but there was nothing to say. I felt as though I had swallowed a heavy stone and that it had lodged halfway down my throat.

"Françoise, this is your brother, and you will meet him someday," Mathilde said softly, "so you should greet him now."

I went to my mother and kissed my brother's shiny head, and she smiled at me a little. So I kissed her too, on her lank, matted hair, and then both of us looked at Mathilde as if she might tell us what was expected of us now.

And then we heard my father crying as he had never cried before. He cried often, ordinarily, but it was just the liquor running out of him through the eyes. This was a deep, hard sound, and my mother set her face down into the baby's head to hide herself from it, and Mathilde got up and shut the door, so we could not see him anymore.

The next day, we buried my brother in the cold earth. It was not yet frozen, so we could dig a grave, and Louis, who was clever with his hands, made a small pine coffin. Mathilde swore that she'd baptized the baby before he died, dribbling water over his head and giving him a good saint's name—Christophe, patron saint of travelers, for he must travel very far. But all the same the priest would not take the walk to say anything over him, and so the only people who cared that Christophe had been in the world at all were myself, my father, my mother, and Louis and Mathilde, who both came and held my mother up on either side, for she was very weak. My father stood by me, his face empty of anything that I could see, and we shoveled the dirt over the box. Mathilde and Louis brought a hare that Louis had trapped, and Mathilde made us all a good stew, and we ate together, Mathilde spooning the food into my mother's mouth as though she'd been her own child, though Mathilde's children (four sons and two daughters, all living and hearty) were grown up and gone.

That night, my mother slept sound, her eyes red and swollen. I sat by the kitchen fire, eating nuts, knowing that I must get up to try at least to finish the washing—for nothing stops, even for death. Still, I feared that my legs would not hold me, not after that day.

"Françoise."

My father stood over me in the doorway from the bedroom, his hands clutching something to his chest. At first I thought it was the coiled belt with which he sometimes beat me, but only when he was deep in drink, and his eyes were clear and steady now. I saw, peering closer, that it was a book, the only one he owned. A long time ago, in his village in France, the priest had taught him to read, which was a great pride to him, as his parents were unlettered, and his wife, and me too.

"Yes, Papa?"

He sat heavily down, and seemed to not know how to speak to me.

"What is it?"

He sighed.

"It is a great thing, reading," he said, shyly, "a great thing for a man. A man has most use of it. And I thought, always—well, I always thought to have a son, and that he should read. But with so many babies in the earth, I think now that there is only you for me. I will not have a son who will live after me, and know what it is to read. Father François, for whom you are named, gave me this long ago. The Bible, Françoise, and he taught me to read from it."

"I know. You have told me often," I said, turning my face away. I did not want to be pitied for a lack I did not feel. I was as much as any boy, even if I could not read.

"I know I have not been as I should. I have had many burdens."

I shifted again, hearing the familiar pathetic note, and he went on hastily.

"I should like to teach you to read. I am not a scholar, or a priest, or any kind of great person, in the old world or the new one, but I would like—if you are to be my only child to live after me—I should like that you would know what it is to read. I would like that very much. I have not had much good from books, or much knowledge of them, but Father François often spoke of the great love he had of reading. Not only the Holy Book, Françoise, but all kinds of books. He told me that the world is full of books, and stories, and the learning of people. And I have thought sometimes of that, and what it means."

He paused, looking at the book in his hands.

"I know reading is not much good to a woman, at least not to the woman you will be and the place you will have in the world, but who knows what good it will do you. I was always told that a learned woman is no use to anyone. Yet these things were said in France, and we are not there. You could work for the Grey Nuns, Françoise, and read to the old sisters who are blind, and maybe, after I was dead, someone would say, 'There is the daughter of Antoine Laurent, and she knows how to read.' I like to think that may happen."

I was curious, and angry, but more curious than angry now. In truth, I had often wondered about his book and wished to know what it said, and wished to know how to form the letters of my own name. And I had not known how to ask him to teach me, for I was a girl, and one more mark of how he had failed.

And underneath both curiosity and anger, there was a pain in me, for I was no fool. I knew this was the closest he would come to telling me he loved me, so I would do well not to scorn it, however clumsy it was. I would not work for the Grey Nuns, and I would disown him and his ways as soon as I was old enough to escape this house, but to say that would be cruel, and he had had so little kindness in his life.

"Show me, then. Show me how to read the words."

And he opened the book and began aloud.

"We brought nothing into this world, and it is certain we can carry nothing out."

And then he showed me the letters that made those words, marching like ants across the page, one by one.

Chapter Four

"You have to hold it straight," I hissed, moving Marie's hand. "You have to see the three candles lit behind your head. It won't work otherwise."

"Then what?"

"Then you have to ask to see the vision in the mirror, stupid. Like I told you. It should be at midnight, really, under a full moon in a field somewhere, but at least it's dark."

Marie's eyes were wide. Isabelle hugged herself in fear, keeping her reflection well away from my mirror, having no liking for this game. Credulous as geese, both of them, but I needed three people to make my charm work. I only wished they were braver, as brave as I was. I did not fear anything the mirror might show me.

Two seasons had passed since my father had begun to teach me how to read. I had learned quickly, making him as proud of me as he could bear to be. I was a quicker reader than he was now, and had shot up to overtake his height. I was tall and thin and strong, hauling the clothes about with a practiced hand. My parents were still more wedded to the bottle than to each other, as weighed down with stillborn babies and unpaid debts as they ever were, but I had changed much.

The grass had grown on my brother's grave, and in the spring I laid flowers there, thinking of his small body shrunk down to the bones. I felt a sadness sometimes, thinking of him and all the others before him in the earth, but the thought of my brothers and sisters also made me feel stronger. Surely I must be meant for some peculiar destiny, if I alone had survived among them all. Surely there must be a marvelous fate waiting for me.

Marie and Isabelle had come to play games that would show us husbands, because it was Midsummer's Eve. The passing seasons that had made me harder, bolder, more ready for whatever the world might bring seemed to have done the opposite for them. They had no guts at all these days, at least none that I could see. They were both pale and bloodless-blond, with red-rimmed, timid eyes. Lately, they made me want to scare them silly, and I knew it would not be very difficult.

"You have to hold it carefully," I told Marie, whose hand had slipped again, "so it shows us our three reflections and the three candles. Isabelle, come out of that corner or you will spoil everything."

"But I'm afraid."

"Coward. Do you want to be married or not?"

"Yes."

"And to a fine husband, a merchant even, from France or England, with great warehouses and many men working for him, yes?"

"I won't marry an Englishman for all the gold in France. Heretics, all of them, and they will burn in hell forever, my mother says."

"And you always listen to your mother, don't you? Do you want a good Catholic then, who's kissed the Pope's ring himself, and sleeps on a mountain of gold, and could buy and sell all of New France and never feel it?"

"Yes."

"Well, come out of the corner or I swear all you'll get is a walleyed peddler so simple he pisses into the wind. I can tell the future, so I know."

"Liar!" said Marie, showing some unexpected spirit.

"I might be. Then again, I might not be. Why take the chance?"

Silence from both of them. Then, Isabelle slowly shifted herself so all three of us could be seen in the mirror, with the candles behind. Though we stood in the modest kitchen, in the mirror the shadows thrown by the candles seemed vast. The jumble and mess of the dirty room, the sheets hanging from the rafters, all took on a strange aspect. It was a very hot night, with the muffled stillness of summer heat. In the mirror, we looked pinched and lost, with the kitchen spreading out behind us, full of cobwebs and dark corners.

I made my face serious and stern, and spoke in a hush so they had to lean in close to hear me. I was making it all up out of my head, and I had to work quickly, for my mother was asleep next door, and my father might come home at any time.

"A woman lives in the mirror. She was a bad woman in her life, and she was punished by the Holy Virgin, who sent her to live deep in the world on the other side of the mirror. Inside the mirror, everything is different. It is winter there always, and the trees are covered with ice. It is a terrible forest in the mirror, and she lives among the icy trees. Everything is silver, except the woman. She is white as snow, and she has no blood left in her veins, so she does not feel the cold. She is dressed always in black, black silk and lace, for she killed her husband, and so she mourns for her dreadful crime. And in her mourning she weeps tears of blood. But by the grace of the Holy Virgin—"

I paused and crossed myself dramatically. They did the same. Isabelle's hands shook. I looked them both in the eyes in turn, widening my own eyes as if in fear.

"By the grace of the Holy Virgin she was permitted to show to young girls a vision of their future husbands, on Midsummer's Eve, and so over many long years earn her way into heaven. But you must ask in the right way, for she is capricious. And if you do not—"

I paused again, and dropped my voice to the barest whisper.

"If you do not, if you offend her, if you speak her name too loudly, if you quaver before her, or if you are too bold as well, then she will come out of the mirror, she will claw her way out of the mirror, she will grab you and drag you into the mirror with her, she will pluck out your eyeballs, you will live in the mirror with her forever, you will weep tears of blood in the mirror, and there will be no husband then, or anything else. The mirror-world is full of the ghosts of girls who did not please her. They all stand behind her, hundreds of them, weeping shadows with no eyes. Now. Are you ready?"

"Yes," said Marie. I smiled at her, thinking perhaps she had more blood in her than I had supposed. Isabelle nodded, her face drawn and tense.

"We must all look hard into the mirror—don't cast your eyes down, Isabelle, or we're all done for—and we must all say together, now repeat this after me: I humbly petition—"

"I humbly petition—"

"With open heart—"

"With open heart—"

"And by the grace of the Queen of Heaven—"

"And by the grace of the Queen of Heaven—"

"To see the face of my future husband."

"To see the face of my future husband."

We were all quiet then, watching our own eyes staring back at us from the mirror. I made my breath come gasping, and trembled as I spoke.

"Look! Look! I see her! I see the woman! Look there! She weeps bloody tears. She has on a beautiful dark veil, she holds her hands up to her cheeks, her cheeks are white as milk, and her eyes are only pupils. Ah, her hands have long nails like claws, her hands are thin and white as bleached bone. Hold still, she will show us the vision."

"I can't *see* anything," said Marie, trying to hold the mirror steady. "I can't see her."

"That's because you have no faith. Look, look how she sobs!"

They both looked hard at the mirror, which showed them nothing but our three faces and the candles. I went on. "And now she smiles at me, she beckons to me, look, she beckons me with her finger! She is telling me that I am chosen, I will find a husband."

"Why you?" Marie asked, her voice barely a whisper. "Why not me?"

Isabelle began to cry, though whether from fright or the thought of being a spinster, I could not tell.

"Don't cry, stupid! She will see it and be made angry. I must watch to see my husband."

I stared into the mirror, with furrowed brows. I would laugh in a minute, I knew, so I decided it must be finished.

"No, no, she reaches her arms toward me—she is reaching out of the mirror—help me—"

And then I screamed, shrill and long, covering my eyes from the mirror.

I put out my hands and caught it just in time, for I had frightened both sisters out of their wits and Marie had let my precious mirror fall from her hand. They backed away from me, screaming louder than I had, and then both turned and ran pell-mell out the door, still shrieking like hags. They passed my father, who was finally stumbling home, his jacket on askew, his hat perched sideways on his head, singing a dirty song. He stopped in his tracks, his mouth open in a foolish round, bewildered by the two figures hurling themselves out into the night, toward the safety of their own house. Standing in the doorway, I laughed to see his befuddlement, but I laughed only inside myself, not wanting to make him angry, for I feared his anger as I did not fear any women who might live in my cracked mirror.

"What have you been doing, Françoise, to make them shriek so? Setting their hair on fire?"

"No, Papa, only telling them tales."

"Well, if they are too frightened to hear a tale, they'll get little pleasure of life. Are you sure that was all you did?"

"I swear. I only told them stories, and if they behave like fools, well, it is not my fault."

My father grinned uncertainly at me, and belched.

"That's my girl, Françoise. Let the fools be fools. Fools! All the world is made up of fools! All of New France is full of fools! Fools and scoundrels, cheating honest men of their money!" And he waved his arms vaguely about his head, as if swatting at flies. I wondered how much he had even heard me.

"Did you lose at cards again, Papa?" I asked.

"Cheated! Cheated by foul rogues! They do not play fair! Cheats! Cheats!"

I sighed. He would work himself into a rage now, and I had no wish to be up with him all night, getting him sober.

"But how are we to pay it, my girl? How are we to ever be clear?"

"Do not mind it, Papa. Go to bed. We will figure out what

you owe in the morning, and how it might be paid."

He swayed on his feet.

"Help me up the stairs then, my good girl. My old bones are not meant for climbing."

It was two steps up to our door. I went and hoisted his arm across my shoulders.

"There we go, Papa, easy does it. Up we go."

Helping him through the kitchen I heard my mother stir in our bedroom, just waking out of a heavy sleep. I helped my father with his boots, and quieted her, and having put both my charges to bed I sat at the table for a while in the darkness, having blown out the three candles.

I thought about words. Words, it seemed, were power, even for those with nothing in the world. I had made Marie and Isabelle fear and tremble before a phantom, before nothing but their own reflections. Words had done that. Words could make things true, conjure things that had no existence. I thought that was a useful thing to know. Perhaps words could be a way out, for I knew I must find a way out of this life somehow, and not through a husband, though I should not mind one if it was someone I liked in himself. Every girl I knew thought a husband was the way out of the life she had, and every woman I knew seemed to have found it was not so, beginning with my own mother.

I would find some other way out. I would find what my parents could not, and be one that did well in this new land, though how and by what road, I could not see.

Still, the thought made me tingle all the same, for the power I had and the future I would see for myself in the mirror.

Chapter Five

After that, Marie and Isabelle did not like me much. In the light of the next morning, they knew they had been taken for fools and that nothing had ever waited in the mirror. When I saw Marie up ahead on the road into town, she walked quicker to keep away from me when I called her name. I was sorry then, for I had not meant to lose their company. But the triumph of the trick was greater than the loneliness.

It was the mid-end of summer, which was a dangerous time in Montreal, especially in the sloped huts like ours, where there was never enough to eat. Summer meant heat and stink, maggots in the meat, ferment in the cider, white worms and weevils all about. The smell in those hot days could make your head swim, so mixed up it was with rot, spoiled food, dirty clothes. Every scrap of cloth clung to our skins, and we could not stand the smell of ourselves. Sweat dripped into my eyes, and the buzz of drowsy insects was always in my head. I felt crazed, and saw that same feeling on every face I met. Everything seemed to bubble and boil in the sweat of July, and even the breeze off the water was no help.

Then August came, bringing sickness.

I heard of it early, skulking about the market. Though I still had an eye for loose vegetables, I had not seen the red-haired boy all summer, nor his father. I wondered idly sometimes where the boy was, and if he would remember me to see me. The cut above my eye had faded and disappeared to nothing, but sometimes I wished I had a scar; it would have marked my triumph. These days I had more of an eye for bright ribbons than for vegetables, which was a more hopeless longing, as the peddler never let those fall. Though after my brother died, he gave me a length of blue ribbon that had got stained, and I wore it in my hair, the only colorful thing I owned. So I leaned in close to the peddler, eyeing his wares, and heard him gossiping with a servant girl no older than myself, who had come to buy ribbons to trim a cap for her mistress.

"It came in the night," the girl said as she fingered a length of bright red silk, "and the house is in an uproar, their cook told me. She had to shout it to me, for I would not let her come near. All fevered they are in that house—the mistress and the master and two of the children and one of the servingmen—all too sick to walk, and their skin is all pockmarked."

And the peddler spat, and crossed himself.

We were all afraid of the pox, of course. To hear my mother tell stories of Paris, you'd think not a day went by without people dropping dead in the streets, and she said her friends would wear patches and cover themselves with powder to hide the scars they had so the gentlemen would come near them. My mother had never taken sick though, which was a good thing, she said, for she would never have been let on the ship if she'd been pitted up like some women she knew. "Like a grater," she would say, "or as if the skin had been flayed off them, poor things, and it never went away, even when the fever left them. They do not let such women come to New France. It would spoil the colony."

When she told me those stories, I would touch the skin on my face, feeling it smooth and unbroken, and thank my stars I had been born in this new place, with fewer people to carry such sicknesses from door to door. Still, it would come all the same from time to time, tearing through the town like a guilty secret—the burning fever of smallpox, leaving a few dead behind, mostly children and the old, and a few faces scarred forever. The height of summer was the worst time.

But I had other matters in my mind just then, watching that servant girl. She was no handsomer than I was, and shorter, and did not look as strong. Yet she was a maid to the wife of a merchant, and her dress was a soft cloth, and black ribbons were tying up her brown hair.

"Not these," she said airily, tossing the red ribbons down, "for Madame Pommereau thinks such things are vulgar, and not fit for a married woman."

"Well, she may think as she pleases, but these are the finest I have, and quite new, brought in from Quebec only a week ago," he grumbled, folding up the red ribbons carefully.

"I know when the order came in, for she orders them direct and does not buy from you. But somehow her order was not there, so she sent me here. Black, or brown, or maybe blue, but not red. Enough to trim two caps and the collar of her morning gown."

She smiled and touched the red again before he put it away. I wanted to touch it as well, and hovered, wishing I was brave enough to speak. I tugged at the blue ribbon in my own hair.

"If I were as rich as she, I would buy the red. I would wear red ribbons every day of the week!" I said too loudly, trying to make her look up at me.

She smiled complacently as the peddler wrapped up brown and black ribbons, and kept her eyes down.

"That is because you are not a lady, like her, and cannot see why such things will not do."

As she turned away from the peddler with her package in her pocket, I swung round and faced her, and she jumped. But then I did not know what to say, for it was easy for me to be strong and dirty, but much harder to ask simple questions. I could have stolen her purse with no compunction, but I could not get enough spittle in my mouth to make words.

"Yes? What do you want?"

"Your cap, if I know anything," put in the peddler, chuckling, "and the stockings from your legs as well. That girl is fierce as a wasp."

"Let me pass, then," she said nervously, perhaps imagining I would put a knife to her throat in the middle of the square. She stepped sideways quickly, but I stepped with her.

"How does …"

And I could not think how to go on.

"What?"

"How can …"

"Let me pass! My mistress will scold me if I keep her waiting."

"I want to do what you do."

She laughed, wrinkling up her snub nose.

"How can I do as you do?"

"Well," she said, considering me, "you could wash your ears and fingernails better, for one."

I looked down, blushing, at my dirty and broken nails, and then, looking up, I saw she was sorry.

"But you most need someone to recommend you. To say you've got a good character, and can work, and so forth. My uncle wrote me such a letter. He sells tea and keeps an apothecary shop."

"What kind of work?"

"Oh, whatever your mistress asks, anything she asks, the minute she asks it. My mistress says a good maid is like a shadow, always there in back. Really, I think a maid is meant to know what her mistress wants before she knows it herself, but that is sometimes difficult."

She laughed again, pleased, I could see, to feel gracious and superior.

"It's no great mystery, my work. She's lazy as anything, having a maid all to herself and never seeing the inside of her own kitchen. All I've to do is care for her, for the place is crawling with servants to do everything else. As for me, it's just fetch and carry. Mend and sew. Listen to her talk. And I get her old clothes too."

She smoothed down the bodice of her dress, which was

white and brown, with yellow stitching round the hem and cuffs. Unable to help myself, I touched the skirt, and she jumped away from my fingers and passed by me, calling over her shoulder, "Get yourself clean and get yourself a letter of good character, and see who needs service. There will always be some ladies that still believe themselves in Paris and need a servant girl to lace them up and unbuckle them, for they can't lift a finger for themselves. Some ladies don't even know how to put on their own shoes."

And she rounded the corner, her hair shining in the sun.

A maid, I thought, walking home. Fetch and carry, hear and obey. It was not the vision that I still sometimes had before sleep, of myself in silk, sweeping from a carriage into a clean and solid house of gray stone, with everyone watching me in awe, their mouths agape at my new finery. But it was a step on the way, much nearer than I was.

In the kitchen, I astonished my mother by scrubbing my nails and washing my ears, tying my hair up out of the way with my stained blue ribbon. Then I took out my mirror and looked into it. My face was flushed with the effort I had put into scrubbing, and my cheeks and nose shone pink. My eyes were bright, whether from hope or desperation I could not tell. I might do, I thought. I might do well enough to get out. And I wished so hard that I might get away from this place, I thought my bones would crack with wishing.

"Your father should never have given you such a gift, for it'll do you no good, and you'd best not grow vain, my girl. Your face will never be your fortune."

"Nor was yours, Mama, yet it got you from France to here." I slipped the mirror back in my pocket.

"That was not so much my face."

"True enough. But I would not speak so frank, if I were you. It's nothing to be proud of."

"Or to be ashamed of. It got me here, and so got you here too, in a manner of speaking." She sighed. "I was not brought up to virtue. The closest I ever got to it was those Quebec nuns. Perhaps I should never have left them."

I waited for a litany of her woes, beginning with my father, but instead she leaned into me and pinched me lightly on the cheek.

"And yet it was good I did, in a way. For here you are. You'll never get beyond this house, my poor girl, not in your rags. But I should not jeer at you for making your face and hands neat. You look very well, indeed. You do me credit."

Before I could say anything, she commenced sneezing into a pile of clean linen, and I moved the pile away, for she was sneezing with great force, and gasping hard for air. Her breath had been short, the last few days.

Standing with my arms full of sheets, I surveyed the kitchen. Three chairs, all broken and mended in some way, a table scattered with our dented pewter plates and cups with the crumbs and smears of our breakfast still on them, another table loaded with clean and dirty cloth, the stained chopping board and washboard. The sight of myself washed clean had made my heart leap, for it was a face that might do anything. But the room called me back to what I was. The room, my mother and her dripping nose, the buzz of the flies made sluggish by the heat, were so far from the prim neatness of that maidservant that she might have been a creature from another world. I might wish, but there was no escape.

But a wish is a dangerous thing. A wish is powerful and terrible.

I sat up with my mother all that night, for she burned with fever. She lay in bed, her face flushed and her breath labored, with a curious rash on her arms and her face, spreading down her neck and disappearing below her nightdress. Her eyes, when they opened, were reddened with swollen lids, and rheumy, so it seemed she was weeping. And her body shook with coughing that started light and went on and on until she could not breathe, and she wheezed, flushed and frightened. It was a rustling, dry sound, that cough, and it made me think of small stones and leaves rattling around inside her chest. She cried that the light of the candle hurt her eyes, and so I blew it out and watched her in the darkness, with only the moon to show me. My father sat up also by her side, on the little stool, and stroked her hand. He was so gentle with her that I wondered, looking back later, if he knew.

In the morning I went for Mathilde.

"It's the pox, isn't it?" I asked Mathilde as she bent over my mother. She chuckled.

"Not the pox, by any stretch," she said, wringing out the cold cloth. "Nor is it in the house in town that silly girl spoke to the peddler of, for all your saying. It's measles, my dear, which can be hard going, but not nearly so bad. See there? No mistake."

She pulled back my mother's cracked lips to show me the inside of her cheek, which was covered with tiny blue-white spots.

"Measles, and nothing else. Rest easy, Françoise. We'll soon get her well."

She turned and squinted at my father, the corners of her mouth turned down.

"But you, Antoine, you get to bed as well and sleep. You look fogged in, and you're sober, by your breath. I'd say you are not well either."

He obeyed. Anyone who had even a scrap of sense did as Mathilde told him.

After she had seen them both under covers, she found me in the kitchen, peeling potatoes, for I thought it best to feed her at least for her pains. She closed her hands over my own and made me put down the knife. Then she turned me round to face her.

"Françoise, go to my house and stay there. I've had it already, and I'm tough as a tree anyway. Old bones. But you should get out of here. When you get there, change your clothes. You will find a dress and underclothes in the trunk beside the bed. Louis will show you. Leave your own clothes in a pail of water outside the house. I'll be along when I can."

I felt awkward in Mathilde's old dress. It fit me well

enough, for she was thin and wiry too. It was patched and faded, but a soft gray, and better than my own clothes. Still, it was not mine, and I wanted to be in my house. Louis sat beside me on their front steps, and got me to help him clean and fix his tools, for there was little else for me to do. The heat made the air shimmer round us. I thought about cool water, and rain; I thought of snow, and I wished my head did not ache. Louis was no great talker, saying only once, softly, that all would be well, by God's grace.

About dinnertime, we saw a figure coming down the path. At first, I thought it was Mathilde, to tell me that my parents were better and that I might go home again, but it was Marie, carrying a basket. We stared at each other and then she looked away.

"I came to see you." She came and set the basket down on the step.

"Why did you want to see me?"

"To say I was sorry. For running away when you saw me on the road. I don't want you to think… I don't mind about the game. It was a mean trick, but I don't mind so much now."

"I shouldn't have done it." And I started down the stairs toward her, meaning to hold out my hand to show I wished us to be friends again, but she stepped away.

"Don't come any nearer. I'm sorry. My mother said to not get near. I haven't had it."

She saw confusion in my face.

"I went to see you, but Mathilde came out and said to tell

my mother your parents are very sick, and can she send over some food, and food for you and Louis too. So she has sent it. There it is." And she nudged the basket with her toe.

"That was great kindness," Louis said, bowing slightly. "Please tell your mother that was a great kindness."

"But my mother says I can't stay to eat it, because none of us have had it, in case you're sick too. So I'm to leave it and come home. Many in the town are sick, too, my mother's heard, but she did not think it would spread to us."

But she hovered. "Françoise?"

"Yes?"

"When your parents are better, can you come to see me?"

I grinned.

"But I promise not to conjure up any bloody women in the mirror this time."

She laughed. And then, quick, as if making it quick could make it not have happened, she put her hand on my arm and leaned close and said, "Don't fret. It will work out for the best."

And then she went.

❧ ❧ ❧

I stayed four days with Louis. I slept on a straw pallet on the floor, that he dug out for me from the woodshed and set up in a corner of the kitchen. It was a kingdom of fleas. I lay there scratching in the dark and breathed in the rank warm smell of dead skins, and watched the moonlight moving over the pots and kettles. In the day, I helped him with his work, and we were both silent.

The hours were slow, the sun crawled along the sky, and the nights were stifled and anxious. I thought often of the fragile length of my mother, my father's more solid bulk. Sometimes I was fearful, and sometimes, guiltily, I thought that being without them would make me free. I pushed that thought down deep inside myself.

I did not love them, that was the truth. Or half-truth, for of course I did love them, because they were all I had ever known. And both things existed side by side, splitting me in two.

Every night, Louis would pat my arm and say that all would be well, just as Marie had said. And I wasn't sure if he could see in my face that I did not know what that would mean for me.

On the morning of the fifth day, I saw Mathilde, stumping along the road. She walked heavy and slow. I ran so fast the dust flew out behind me. When I got to her she told me, her voice harsh, to stay back until she had burned the clothes she stood in. So I moved away from her and we stood, hovering together on the path.

"It is a shame, Françoise. I did as well as I could. I am sorry." And she looked down, and her face was tired, and very old. I looked down too, because I could not look at her and did not know what I should say.

Chapter Six

The army paid for the double funeral. There was a priest, at this one.

We gathered in the church, and I fixed my eyes on the wooden image of Our Lady of Good Help at the altar. I wondered how she could help me, but was too tired to know how to ask. The carved figure had traveled long ways from France, wrapped in a white cloth by sister Marguerite, who common women whispered should be made a saint. I thought of Marguerite, dead and buried now, like the last of my own kin would soon be. She had been a teacher, she had made the crossing and founded a school and built this church, and she was held up to young girls as a great example. But I did not want her to be my example. I did not wish to teach snot-nosed brats and sleep always on a hard bed.

Mathilde nudged me in the ribs, and whispered that I should pray to Marguerite, though she was not a saint yet. I thought that Marguerite was just old bones in the church-yard, like all the dead. I did not say that to Mathilde, but rather bowed my head and moved my lips obediently, and out of the corner of my eye I saw her nod pious approval.

In the graveyard, the fresh hole yawned wide, the earth thrown around it rich and brown, teeming with worms and insects.

As the coffins were lowered, the priest stood over the grave, intoning passionately—"We brought nothing into this world, and it is certain we can carry nothing out"—and I saw the old commander purse his thin lips so they almost disappeared into his face. He was an upright old man, of perfect manners and dignity, with grimly self-satisfied eyes. His hands shook a little, and his uniform lent him the only color he had. If I had met him alone on the road at night, I would have taken him for the ghost of an old campaigner, from some battle long ago. The most he'd ever had to do with my father was to punish him for having dirty boots, cuffing him under the ear like a small boy and not a grown man who could suffer hurt pride.

I could see he thought the priest's delivery undignified, and he flinched visibly as the Holy Father lifted his eyes to heaven and implored that Our Lady would intercede for these poor sinners. Perhaps the commander thought the priest should not harp on sin, given who he was burying. I thought, without of course saying, that the priest probably had no idea who lay in those two rough pine coffins. He'd had to hold so many funerals in the last week. Measles, and not the pox (Mathilde was right, no surprise there), had swept the town, and the streets stank of death and smoke, hanging low in the heat. All sheets and clothes that had touched the sick were burned. There was no rain.

I was pleased that it was a crowded funeral. All the men had turned out in their fine coats, and their buttons and boots shone. The women hung behind in small groups, their voices a steady fluttering sound under the words of the priest. They seemed to me nervous and mean-spirited, except Mathilde, who stood still and kept her hand resting lightly on my arm.

Yet I could see they all thought me very dignified as I stood dry-eyed and quiet. I heard the soldiers' wives, my mother's old cohorts, whispering that the Laurent girl was brave. But inside I was only cold and my mouth felt as though I had swallowed sand. I remembered my father, teaching me to read with those same words the priest had said, and my mother calling me a good girl, and though I knew her voice was bleared with drink as she said it, and that he wished I had been a son, my memory softened these things until I had to look away from the grave at my own feet in their unfamiliar shoes. Every scrap I wore was borrowed, for I had no clothes fit for that day.

As the last handful of earth was flung on the coffins and the gravedigger took up his spade to finish the work, a great sigh and whispering began, louder than before. The soldiers and their women broke into little clumps all about, glancing at me furtively from time to time. I could not hear what it was they said, exactly, for they kept their voices low. But I knew all of it tended to the same question: What shall be done with Françoise?

"What will you do now?" Marie asked that night, sitting on one of our wobbly kitchen chairs. Isabelle perched on a stool beside and I stood by the window, looking out into the yard. They had come with food, and stayed to eat most of it, for I had little appetite.

"I heard Mama say to Mathilde that nothing can be done for you. Your luck is so bad, you're near cursed, and it is a shame," Isabelle said. "Do you think it is true?"

"Even if it were, your mother is a stupid cow to say so, and you can tell her that from me."

Isabelle opened her mouth but Marie clutched her arm.

"Don't *fight*, either of you. It makes my head hurt. Isabelle, you have called our mother a cow yourself often enough, so let it pass."

I turned to face them both. Their eyes were wide. I saw that neither really knew what to say, and that it made them harsh from fear of me.

"Perhaps I will go and live in the woods and eat roots and berries, and not trouble anyone anymore."

Marie slid off the chair as if she meant to comfort me somehow, then thought better of it and sat down again.

"You could get married, and then it would be settled."

"Who'd marry *her*?" Isabelle muttered, jutting her jaw in my direction.

"Don't look like that, Françoise, but see sense. You cannot stay here alone, with nothing to eat and nothing to do. You'd be wild as a bear within a week in this mess."

She looked around. I had not had the heart to set the house to rights, and it was in a state, with old food and flies and sheets tumbled about, and on a shelf, my mother's uncorked bottle. It looked as though my parents had left suddenly, and would soon return. Tidying away all trace of them would make them truly gone. Perhaps I would stay here, in their filth, and my hair would get matted and I would begin to talk to myself and throw things out the window at any who tried to approach my door.

"Come, you look nearly pretty in all that black, with your hair combed. We could find you a trapper or some such, if he wasn't too fussy, couldn't we, Isabelle?"

"Save yourself the trouble. I wouldn't have a trapper. Marry a trapper yourself, if that's what you want. I have other things in mind."

I spoke bravely, but my voice caught a little. This time Marie did get up from her chair, and began to clear the table of the plates and old crusts of bread.

"Leave it!"

She jumped.

"I am sorry, Marie, but leave it. Do not touch my house, or counsel me. I won't have it."

She sat, looking at me curiously.

"All right, but what will you do? If a trapper is not good enough for you?"

I stuck out my jaw just as Isabelle had, and spoke with a confidence I did not feel.

"I will go and be a maid to a fine lady, and wear good clothes, and eat meat every day of the week."

The astonishment in both their faces made me want to laugh. Then both began to laugh themselves, long and shrieking, Marie at first trying to hide her face in her hands, and Isabelle beating her fists upon the table, choking with glee. And I lowered my head, shamed.

❄ ❄ ❄

"What should be done with Françoise?"

It was the next night, and it was Toinette who spoke this aloud. I had been sitting, gnawing on some leftover bits and pieces of food, blessedly alone at last and beginning to feel some ease in my own skin. Then all at once a pack of women had descended on the kitchen, all the well-meaning bustling soldiers' wives who could not leave anything alone. Their eyes were bright with sympathy and purpose. Last of all came Mathilde, and her face was grim. I could tell she did not think much of these ladies and their good intentions. She went and stood in the corner out of the fuss, but kept her eyes fixed on me. The other women clumped themselves about the room, clucking their tongues at the dirt, for I still had not lifted a finger.

Toinette was an old whore herself, like my mother. But unlike my mother, Toinette was stout and hearty, and had borne five big sons for her husband, who drank little and never lost at cards.

All the voices broke over me at once. The women spoke

loudly, eagerly, taking charge of the room while I stood quietly looking down, knowing nobody expected me to speak.

"Perhaps she could apprentice—"

"That new seamstress seeks a girl, she told me so herself, to help with the sewing orders for the winter, perhaps arrangements could be made—"

"That's no life for the poor thing. She's a hard woman. Françoise would be half-blind by next spring. She'd make her sew at night with only one candle. My daughter was there but I had her home again before the month was up, and she was half-starved."

"But surely anything is better than what she is used to. Look at her—she's skin and bone as it is."

"All the more reason to keep her from that place. She'd not last."

"Has she no family at all? No one?"

"Not that anyone knows, but perhaps in France?"

"We cannot send her back to France. Who'd pay for it, I'd like to know? Who could arrange it? We cannot get her on a ship before the last ones sail in October."

"Does no one wish to marry her?"

Silence. All turned and looked pointedly at me.

"No," I whispered.

"Well, she's young still, and goodness knows she's had little chance, living in this hut with such parents, so let us not worry about that yet, it is not our business," said Toinette, patting my arm dismissively.

"God rest them," said Mathilde, from where she stood in the corner, and "God rest them," caroled all the other ladies, devoutly.

Silence again. And in the silence I felt a spark of anger in myself at these well-meaning women thinking to settle my life for me.

"Well," said Toinette briskly, as if to settle the matter, "to me it seems plain. She's trained to the laundry, it's in her blood, and hopefully that's all that's in her blood. The kettles and such are already here, and she knows the trade well, is that not so? The house is a disgrace now, Françoise, to be sure. But you shall make it clean and neat, as a God-fearing girl must do, and everything will be well."

She faced the room now, a smile of satisfaction spread over her face.

"I think we may call that final. Let her continue her mother's work. We will all send her our custom. She is young, but with hard work, which she's suited for, she can do very well, and with our things to wash, she'll soon be in a fair way to making her proper living. I shall tell everyone I know: send your laundry to Françoise Laurent. And if she's wise and does not charge too high, she's set up for life. It is not a bad fate, and more than might be expected." And she crossed her arms and beamed at me, as though she'd given me a gift.

I looked down and bit my lip as pleased murmurs ran round the room.

"The very thing. Why did we not think so at once, Toinette!"

"For that way she can be respectable, and not a trouble to anyone."

"It is the most fitting course, for this way she can do honor to her parents and better herself at the same time, for she's more industrious than they. You can see it in her face. Let her wash clothes, and so it is done."

"I will not!"

My voice surprised me and I covered my own mouth, for I had not meant to speak so loud. I had shouted this. They all drew back, astonished.

"I will not," I said again, steadier now, looking up. "I will not be a washerwoman and wash your clothes, or anyone's clothes. I will not be a laundress and slave over the kettles and rub my hands raw with soap. I will beg for my bread in the gutter before that."

"You can't beg for your bread," said Toinette, her voice cold now. "It would disgrace the whole of the army, and us, to have you begging in the streets."

"I will be a disgrace then. I am already. You know it, all of you, though you will not say."

No one met my eye then. I went on.

"You wish me out of the way, but I will not go. I want to be … I want …"

And to my own helpless rage, I found myself crying. It seemed to all rush upon me at once—the crooked hut, the heavy soiled sheets, that I would be the dirty daughter of a dirty mother, washing out other women's secret stains that they were too proud to send elsewhere.

Mathilde faced me and put her hands on my shoulders. She shook me gently.

"Stop it, child, stop. No need for all this fuss. Say what it is, if you want something, and we shall see what can be done."

I stopped crying.

"I wish to be a maid to a merchant's wife, if any will have me."

I could see that some of the women smiled, and some did not know where to look, but just as I wondered if I would hear another chorus of laughter, Mathilde spoke again.

"It's not so unlikely, is it? You're a sharp one, and a bold one, but you learn quick, I must say. And you've got the will to make yourself what is needed, I'm sure. My sister told me yesterday that Madame Pommereau, whose husband has done so well with his furs, needs a maid. Her own maid died of the fever only last week, very sudden it was, and she cannot find another, for all the girls are scared to sleep in the last girl's bed."

The girl at the market, with her ribbons and the yellow stitching on her clean dress. The dress must be burnt up by now, I thought, and her lovely shoes too.

"But Françoise would not be afraid, would you? Not you. You would do nicely. Cannot something be thought on? Cannot something be done?"

I dried my cheeks with my hand, looking at Mathilde's determined face.

Toinette spoke, her eyes hard.

"Do not be a fool. You know much of herbs and babies, but little of the world. Françoise is not fit to scrape the mud from Madame Pommereau's shoes. She would be lucky to be a kitchen maid in that house. Besides, she needs someone to write a letter—someone as grand as the Pommereaus who will vouch for her, and who would? She comes from shameful stock. I know we must not speak ill of the dead, but let us be truthful, all the same. Mathilde, do not meddle in what you do not understand."

As she turned away, a murmur of embarrassed agreement ran round the room. It seemed Mathilde was the only champion I had, and she could not do much for me, in her patched dress, her hands worn and crooked with years of work. I looked down at my own hands and thought how they would grow rough and twisted with years and years of washing.

Mathilde pressed my arm, and shook her head. So that, it seemed, was that.

🕸 🕸 🕸

All the rest of the week I saw no one. I kept the door latched. When Marie and Isabelle came with more food I pretended to be sleeping and they left it on the stairs. Mathilde did not come at all.

I thought sometimes that I should begin to clean the house, to sort the laundry, to set to work on my new life. Food would not be left on the doorstep forever, and those officious women would not send me their washing if I did not stir myself to do it. Yet I could not force myself to do more than eat and sleep, and sit and watch the path that led to our door. Which was not ours anymore, but mine and mine alone. My parents dead, I was as free as a swallow, and at the same time a prisoner, with only one road before me, for such is the way of the world.

Then, one night, someone came pounding at the door. I buried my head deep in the bedclothes, waiting for whoever it was to go away.

"Françoise! Do not keep me standing on the steps, the mosquitoes will suck me dry!"

Hearing Mathilde's voice, I got up.

"Well, ask me in at least!" she said, shifting from foot to foot.

"Come in."

I lit a candle, and in the dim gold light she put something into my hands. Looking down, I saw a folded letter, with the words "For Françoise Laurent" written in a sloping, fine hand above a dark red seal.

"What … what …"

"It's a copy. The other has been sent on to the Pommereau house. You are to take this with you tomorrow, to prove you are Françoise Laurent, and then Madame Pommereau will see you, and if you please her, you shall be her new maid."

"But how—"

"It's from your father's old commander. Toinette may not wish to vouch for you to him, but I have no such scruple, not being the narrow-minded cat she is."

"But how could you …"

I was struck dumb, looking at the letter. It seemed heavy in my hands, the thick expensive paper and loops of ink my way into another life.

Mathilde chuckled.

"It is quite a thing to take away your words, my dear. But this is how it was. I kept turning it over in my mind, all those women washing their hands of you, and you better than any of them. So this morning I took myself off to the commander's house. One of his servingmen let me in. I saved his little son's life last winter and he'd give me the shirt off his back if I asked for it. So he showed me the way into the dining room and I sat down on a fine embroidered chair just as I was, for I am quite as good as they. And I told the commander and his handsome wife—half his age and in a curled white wig, as if she thought she lived in Paris—that I would not stir from the spot until he had written me the letter I wanted. And at first he hemmed and hawed and said he would not take it on. But I would not leave all day and into the evening. I sat in the chair and said they would have to get the soldiers to come and carry me out. I would sit there all night and share their breakfast the next morning if he did not write such a letter as would make Madame Pommereau hire you on the spot. And I told him that you were a good girl, an obedient and gentle girl who will not indulge in any idle talk or vicious habits, and generally told such lies as I am sure will ruin my chances at heaven. So at last he wrote the letter, for he did not know what else to do. And I stayed until he had sent the letter by special messenger to the Pommereau house and given me this one for you, and then I left him in peace. He did as I asked in the end, like a man of honor, so I think well of him, though he looks like he's less blood in his body than a sickly flea, and his wife worse. *She* told him he should call in some rough men and have me thrown out into the street, but he thought it easier to write the letter."

She paused for breath. I still could not speak.

"There now, it's the least I could have done. And it's only an introduction. You still need to make her think you the best she'll ever get. Which I know you are. You have such spirit in you, Françoise. You'll make all of us proud, and go far in the world. I know. I can see it written in your face."

"Thank you, Mathilde," I said, my voice a whisper.

"Don't thank me. But get out of this place. Turn your back on it and never think of it again."

"I will."

I kissed the soft worn leather of her cheek and placed the letter carefully on the table.

"Tomorrow, I will come to help you make ready, and then you will go."

After I had watched her walk down the road and disappear into the night, I sat for a long time at the table, staring at the letter. The curves of my name seemed to flicker and twist in the light from the candle, until the flame guttered and went out.

Chapter Seven

I borrowed a good dress from Mathilde's youngest daughter, scrubbed myself pink and shiny in my mother's copper washtub, and went the way I had been told, the letter clutched in my hand. I held my skirt up high out of the mud and picked my way through the streets toward the Pommereau house, and there I was.

Madame Pommereau looked me over in her dressing room. It was a big room, with the sun coming in from a great window divided by many panes of glass. Those panes cut the light, which played over her face oddly. She wore a white frilled morning cap. To me she seemed all light, her face very pale, her hair under the cap showing faded brown streaked with a few threads of white. She wore a white dress that whispered and rustled as she moved away from the fire screen she was embroidering, no doubt to keep her skin from roughening when she sat by the hearth. The needlework on the screen made a knot in my heart, it looked so fine, and I saw myself callow beside it, wishing to be as good as that thread.

"Stand in the light," she said, not looking at me.

I went and stood closer to the small fire, for it was September now and the air was colder.

"No, there by the window."

She came and stood beside me, looked into my face.

"Yes?" I said.

She frowned slightly, almost a flinch, patting her left hand with her right as if she was scolding her hand in place of me.

"'Yes, Madame,' is how you should address me."

"Yes, Madame."

She softened, seeing my face, and I, seeing her soften, blushed for my own ignorance of all she would want, and so we stood there, me blushing and she suddenly tender at my discomfort. I thought suddenly that I might spark some gentleness in her because she thought me young and simple, and so I tried to look as simple as I could.

"This letter speaks very well of you. Françoise Laurent, age fifteen, of good character and virtue. Mother a washerwoman, father in the grenadier and gunner company, both deceased."

She smoothed out the letter the commander had sent, then lifted one small hand, turning my face so I was full in the light from the window, gravely looked at my profile, let her hand drop.

"You have dirt behind your left ear."

I blushed again. I had tried so hard.

"Your mother was a washerwoman. Did she not teach you to wash?"

"Yes, Madame."

"Don't contradict me, please."

She moved away and sat back by the fire, looking again at the letter.

"It says: biddable, trainable, docile, clean, gentle. Are you?"

"Madame?"

"Are you those things?"

I did not know which way to look.

"Yes."

"Yes?"

"Yes, Madame."

"And not conceited either, I see."

"No, Madame."

And then I thought I might laugh too, to see her face, not knowing whether to be charmed or angry.

"I must train you, of course."

"Yes, Madame."

"There is not much you know, is there?"

I pondered that.

"No, Madame. But what we don't know, we may learn."

"Good answer."

"Madame?"

"I'll take you."

She stood up again, looking me right in the face as if seeing me for the first time. Her eyes were bright blue. I seemed all at once to be finer in her gaze, a promise of something, something even to look forward to.

"I'll take you. After all, what choice do I have?"

I looked down at the floor.

"I have learned to make do here, Françoise."

I was silent, not knowing what she now wished me to say.

She turned away, looking out the window. Outside, the big maple was beginning to turn red.

"Françoise, do you like this place?"

"Where, Madame?"

"Montreal. New France."

"I was born here."

"Then you will teach me how to love it. We always love the place where we are born. Come back tomorrow, at the same hour."

And so I left the house as Madame Pommereau's maid. Françoise Laurent, servant, of good character and virtue.

❧ ❧ ❧

It is not true that we always love the place in which we are born. Going to my old home, having promised to return to the Pommereaus' the next day, I felt the liberty of leaving. I still had the stink of poverty on me, but in Madame Pommereau's house, I thought, I would wash it away.

That night, I packed up my life as it had been. A few stray coins, a few old clothes, the brooch that had been my mother's, one of the only things she had brought from France. Pewter, twisted like a rose, a little blackened now. Then I said my prayers and went to bed hoping to dream of my new life, but I dreamed nothing but darkness, a soft big night with no stars, and somewhere the voices of my parents saying something I could not hear.

In the morning I shut the door behind me and did not even bother to fasten the latch. Anyone could go in who would, for I would never cross the threshold again. And I walked away quickly, not even daring to look back in case I should bring down bad luck on my head, just as my luck was beginning.

Chapter Eight

Though I had thought to sing as I walked to the Pommereau house, I cursed instead under my breath, finding myself late. I hurried along, holding my skirt up out of the way of wagon ruts and dust, afraid to take the back ways I knew so well because they were dirty and unkempt, and so losing my way easily as I rushed down the narrow streets. Carts and horses passed me, cobblestones tripped me, and as the neighborhood grew grander, I was held up by ladies and gentlemen out walking arm in arm, floating lazily along as though nothing in the world had ever vexed them, and every stitch upon their plump bodies clean and new.

I wanted more than anything to appear proper on my first morning. My hair was parted, slicked down with water and tied tight, my fingernails clean and soft, and my eyes shone. In my pocket, my little mirror bounced back and forth, and I was thankful again for it. In spite of the time slipping by, I took it out as I rounded a corner and looked once more at my own face, to make sure nothing was out of place. I stared intent, my head down.

"Watch where you're going!"

In my haste, I ran straight into him, rocking him on his feet. Rubbing my forehead, I looked up into the face of a new recruit, not much older than myself. His face was red from embarrassment at losing his balance and his friends stood around him, laughing, all proud of their new uniforms.

"Careful, now, she's only a girl."

"If that knocks you over, you'll never manage a charge."

"Don't give him a horse, he'd not stay on."

"His first day, and already unseated."

"Get out of my way," he muttered to me, glaring down at his own shiny boots, his hands smoothing out the front of his coat.

I curtsied and stepped aside, trying not to laugh, for I knew, as he walked off with his fine friends, that it was the red-haired boy from the marketplace, only a year ago, and he did not recognize me at all. I whistled, soft, "Oh, the pleasure of love is fleeting, but the sorrow of love lasts," half-hoping he would turn back. But he rounded the corner, his shoulders hunched, his friends still mocking him, a boy among boys. I wondered, briefly, if my father had ever looked so young, so white and thin-skinned, waiting for his life to begin.

In the still-early morning, the long gray house seemed dead, but perhaps this was just that the light was also gray. I could see movement behind some of the many windows (fourteen in all, all diamond paned—I counted them in wonder). The flash of a sleeve, a hand drawing a curtain, someone walking away from the glass and through a doorway into another, unseen room. Drifts of smoke curled up from the double chimneys, high above me, two stories and then the sloping, neatly slated roof. I hovered, not knowing what to do, for there were two main doors and I could not see which one I should go through. Before, a scared-looking kitchen maid had met me on the steps and shown me through, but now there was no one.

I stood before the doors, wondering what I should do next. Then I heard voices. Two men, servants, stood at a side door talking, one polishing a pair of boots, and the other idle.

"Who are you?" asked the first man.

"Must be the new maid," said the other, jutting his chin at me and licking his bottom lip. He was younger than the one who'd spoken first, but his face was all grease and spots. A weasel in a dirty shirt.

"Well, go on then," said the older.

"I don't know the way."

"Not either of those, if you want to last a day. Come through here and see Berthe—she's the cook. She'll tell you how to get upstairs. Come along."

So I pushed past, not thinking much of either of them. I was Madame Pommereau's maid now, and I'd have nothing to do with such men. The younger one winked at me as I went and I winked back. Force of habit—it would be unfriendly not to—but I cursed myself immediately. Madame Pommereau, I was sure, would not want her maid winking.

The kitchen, right inside the door and down four wide steps. Vast, stretching out into dim corners, the walls stone and smoothed plaster, the floor great beams of wood and the ceiling the same. A little strained light from small cellar windows, barred to keep out thieves. And the firelight from the wide dark hearth playing on all that dark wood and from those rafters pots and kettles and skewers and spoons hanging, as if to feed giants. Copper pots and dishes lined shelves all along the walls, all orderly and shining with a dull glow. A good smell wafted up from a pot over the fire, a smell of meat cooking. Heaps of chopped things over a big wooden table made, it seemed, from leftover pieces of the floor. Carrots, potatoes, beets and other roots, all ready for the pot. And at the far end of the table stood a woman who seemed as big and strong as everything else in that place. Bursting at the seams of a stained dress and capacious apron, her bulk straining against the edge of the table, legs and arms like pallid, mottled tree trunks. The cook, bending over a little rabbit that she was skinning with expert hands, letting the blood flow down the draining board and into a yellow mixing bowl. To one side, two other rabbits reduced to wobbling masses without skins. Her red hands working away at the raw red meat made me hungry.

I watched, waiting for her to look up. I was overwhelmed suddenly with the grandeur of my new position, and thought I would do better to work in the kitchen. It was warm and pleasant, even with the knives lining the walls and all the blood running down the table. A seat by the fire, and this creature Berthe as my mistress. But I was late for my true mistress, and I was forgetting all my ambition. My hands would get even rougher with all that chopping and washing and straining and scouring, when I wanted to make them soft and white as doves.

Still no word from the cook.

"Hello?"

She looked up slowly, saw me. Grinned a wary toothless smile and chuckled.

"I'm here to be the new maid to Madame Pommereau."

She put her hands on my shoulders, made a grunting sound in her throat, and I realized with shock that she had no tongue. Still, she smiled and smiled, and then led me to a set of stairs and pointed me up them. A nasty trick those men had played, knowing she couldn't tell me the way.

I climbed the narrow stairs, which ran up and up. The ceiling was low, the walls close on either side. Light spilled round the edges of a shut door at the top. I touched a wall to steady myself and found it was rough plaster, powdery white under my hands. Opening the door, I stepped into what I took to be the upper hallway, very wide and full of dark polished wood, with windows streaming light and a curved staircase leading down to the front entrance I remembered from my interview. Then, I had hurried along to meet Madame Pommereau, the kitchen maid tugging nervously at my sleeve. Now I suddenly forgot my haste and stood gawking, my eyes narrowing in the brightness after the dark stairs. Looking around, I saw a series of doors, all shut. I opened the first one, which led to a room full of high-backed upholstered chairs set in a big half circle by a stone fireplace with little china figures ranged across the top of it, shepherds and shepherdesses whiter and cleaner than any I had ever heard of. It made me smile, that wealthy people should think rustics so simple and sweet. I heard the loud ticking of a clock on the mantelpiece. To my dismay, I saw it was even later than I thought.

I ran back into the hall, opened another door, tripped over my skirt, and nearly fell into what I thought must be a dining room, because there was a big table with a little bald man sitting at it, reading over some papers.

"Yes? What are you doing in my study?"

He blinked at me with damp gray eyes and adjusted a pair of spectacles perched along his long bony nose.

"I'm the new maid. Françoise Laurent. Sir. I've lost my way."

He rose, brushing imaginary crumbs from his long black velvet coat.

"Ah. Yes. My wife is expecting you."

I looked down.

"You are late, I believe."

"It will not happen again, Sir."

"I don't see how it could, as you will be living here with us." Then he smiled.

"Come, don't be afraid. My wife is a woman of some nervousness, and so I wish for her not to suffer upset. I will show you the way. You are in quite the wrong part of the house."

He led me back along the hall, through a doorway that led down another hall, and then, finally, through an open door to the room I remembered. How I had been so turned around, I don't know, but I vowed never to be again. I would learn this house, which looked so square and simple outside, but seemed to have parts. His part, her part, the servants' part. The right stairs, the right doors.

She was sitting by the fire, staring into it. She was wrapped in a warm brown morning gown, loose all round her, and had needlework nearby, and a sewing basket at her little slippered feet, but she seemed to be dreaming. The thread was all tangled in her lap, and her lips moved softly, as if she were singing to herself. Monsieur Pommereau patted my arm to keep me where I was, then went and bent over her very gently, his hand on her shoulder, stroking the cloth.

"My dear."

She looked up at him, seeming all at once to come back into the room from wherever it was she had been. She put her hand over his.

"Your new girl is here."

She rose, gestured for me to come in.

"Françoise. There you are."

And he went out.

I stood awkwardly, not knowing what I should do next. She hovered before me, and also seemed unsure, and I wondered if she was waiting for me to say something. So we stood there, neither saying anything, and she drew the folds of her gown round her and shivered, and I felt a fool.

"I am pleased to begin in your service, Madame," I said at last, and tried a curtsy, too quickly, and when I looked again she was frowning.

"Is something wrong, my lady?"

"It will not do."

"What, Madame?"

"No, it will not do." Her hands fussed about my dress, her brow furrowed in irritation. I looked down at my skirts, confused. She clucked her tongue and stepped back, surveying me. I had a sudden terror that she had changed her mind and in another minute I should find myself turned out, the laughter of the servingmen ringing in my ears as I walked down the street with nowhere to go. I pressed my lips together at the thought.

"Yes, I think it will be just the thing," she went on under her breath, and still not meeting my eye, "and if it is a little short, it is no matter."

And without a glance at me she bustled out into another room that her sitting room opened into. I was left standing on the carpet, in a panic.

She was back a moment later, her arms full of cloth. Finally looking into my face, she started.

"Françoise, what is the matter?"

"I do not know, Madame, for you have not said. Should I go?"

"Go? What do you mean, go?"

"Away, Madame? Do I not please?"

Understanding at last, she smiled, a crooked half-smile with a hint of mockery in it.

"I do not know yet whether you please me or not, but your dress is not fit to be seen. It is worn and patched. Here is another."

And she shook out what she carried. It was long and the cloth was a dull dark brown, but thicker and richer than anything I had worn. The skirt seemed very full to me, all spilling down from her arms, and the bodice was beautifully worked with deep green thread over a loose white shirt with ruffled sleeves. I did feel twice-mended and dingy, looking at it. In one hand she held a little purse or pocket looped with ribbon, which I knew was meant to tie around my waist. I had often envied ladies those funny loose purses, flopping at their sides as if they had no fear of thieves, being innocent as babies.

She put the dress into my hands.

"It is a little worn, but not badly. It belonged to the girl who was my maid before."

I nearly dropped the dress, and she smiled again.

"Don't fear, Françoise, she did not wear it when she was ill. We burned the clothes she wore then. Put this on."

I obediently unbuttoned my collar.

"Not here, you silly girl. We are decent creatures, I should hope. Go into the dressing room and come back when you are ready."

"And what I wear now, Madame? What shall I do with that?"

"Leave it in a corner. Later on it shall be put in the ragbag."

I thought with regret of the dress I wore. Mathilde had given it to me herself, to make me look proper. It seemed a shame to throw away such a generous gift. But I did not see how to contradict Madame Pommereau, and the set of her mouth did not seem open to contradiction.

Shutting the door between us, I looked about her dressing room. It was a big white room, with a bare floor of smooth pine boards that glowed in the sun, which came in through heavy green velvet curtains that were drawn back around the single window. There were a few chairs, and the rest was given over to chests of drawers and a high wardrobe, carved wondrously with flowers and leaves, a great wooden thing as big as a room. Another door at the farthest end of the room was half open, showing me a glimpse of a carved bed, hung with curtains of the same dusty green velvet as the curtains on the windows, and beyond that, another door that was shut but probably opened back out onto the hallway. I marveled at this honeycomb of rooms, all for her to sit in and sleep in and dress in. I had known whole families who lived in quarters smaller than the rug spread out before her fire.

For all the richness of cloth and wood, the dressing room had a sparse, hard look, and the air was stale and chill, the walls bare but for one picture, framed in wood and drawn in hundreds of delicate black strokes. Curious, I stood before it, and saw an image of ladies and gentlemen dancing in an open courtyard before a palace of some kind, with countless stairs and splashing fountains and garlands of flowers hung all about. The ladies wore skirts that made them look like the bells of cathedrals, and the gentlemen had thin spindly legs all swathed in stockings and ribbons, and both wore wigs nearly as high as themselves. I wondered if it was Paris, and somewhere Madame Pommereau had been, and then realized that the picture must be fanciful, for cherubs with trumpets flew over the heads of the dancing crowd, scattering flowers over a fat man who, I saw as I peered closer, must be meant for the king, and very pleased he looked by all the fuss being made of him.

I heard a tap upon the door.

"Françoise? Does the dress fit?"

"One moment, Madame."

I threw off what I wore, tearing the seams in my haste, and laid it over a chair. I drew on the shirt and bodice first, admiring even in my hurry the carved buttons and careful buttonholes, then took it off again, seeing that the skirt was meant to fit under and would not go on last. After much frantic hustle and bustle, I got the whole mass of it on right and was doing up the top buttons and smoothing down the rumpled skirts when she came in, this time without knocking.

"You must learn to be quicker."

"I am sorry, Madame."

She looked me up and down, still frowning, but in concentration.

"It fits you well enough."

And she tugged at the skirt, and showed me how to fluff out the ruffles of cuffs and collar, and to make the bodice fit smooth. Drawing away again, she nodded, a quick jerk of her head.

"That will do, I suppose. Now we will begin."

And she unlaced the morning gown, and stood before me in her shift, and held her hands out stiff to her sides.

"Go and open the wardrobe, Françoise."

And so she began to teach me. There was more to it than I could have imagined. How could one body be cocooned in so many layers of cloth? How could it be so difficult to comb and arrange one head of fine brown hair? What was the sense in wearing clothes with so many hooks and eyes, ribbons and laces that a servant was needed just to get dressed? And where did she go, who saw her, that she must have all this? I had thought myself a clever girl, but I knew nothing, it seemed. My hands, which I had prided myself were as quick as the rest of me, seemed clumsy and strange, afterthoughts to my hapless arms. I was a poor pupil, to begin with.

"Stays?"

"Madame?"

She sighed.

"Françoise, that means I wish you to fetch them. They are hanging there, on the wardrobe wall to your left. Bring them to me, please."

I took down a curled mass of bone and white cloth, worked with hundreds and hundreds of stitches, with long laces hanging from it every which way. I squinted at the thread.

"It would take great skill to sew all that, Madame."

"Yes. Put them on."

I held the stays before me, trying to see which way was up, and where the laces were meant to be pulled. I was not even sure how they were meant to go on. She took them from me, showed me how to hold them to her body, then bent down so I could pull them over her head, and showed my fingers how to pull the laces, how to tie her in.

"These were made in France. They do not have such seamstresses here, Françoise."

"Tell me about France, Madame."

She looked at the floor, her hands still guiding mine.

"Françoise, it is not your business to ask questions. Or to offer opinions. It is not what a maid does."

"What does a maid do then, Madame?"

"Do not be impertinent."

"I did not mean impertinence. I only wish to know, because I do not know and so will make mistakes unless you tell me."

She smiled, seeing I meant it. Her smile was a little wider this time, though I could still see a hint of something harsh in it.

"Well then. Ask."

So I tried again.

"What, then, does a maid do? Madame."

"Well, Françoise … a maid … a maid offers what is needed as soon as it is needed, and dresses me as I please, and carries my things, and talks to me only if I ask her to, and is silent when I want silence. And more than that, as well. A maid is many things. And I wish for you to be a proper maid, not a slatternly kitchen girl who can turn her hand to dressing, such as women have here. But you will learn."

I will indeed, I thought to myself. I looked at both of us in the mirror we stood by. I had never seen myself in a mirror so large. And I could see her beside me. Her skin was creamy white and soft; a whey-faced girl indeed I was next to her. She was shorter than I, and plumper, with a pleasing roundness showing up my angles. But I had pretty wrists and hands, I thought, and good small feet. I had never thought I might be truly pretty before, and it struck me that I would become vain, seeing myself every day like this. She was vain, probably. She had to be, I'm sure, because her body was so petted, so wrapped and cosseted, she could not help but be vain.

She looked in the mirror too, and looked at me in the mirror. She held my eyes, and I thought of the game I played with Marie and Isabelle, by the light of three candles, of the vision of husbands and the weeping bloody woman, and how well I had played it though I had seen nothing there, neither husband nor woman.

"Françoise, you are dawdling. There is much you have to learn, and you waste my time."

So we went on, myself with dogged persistence, and she with a quietly irritated patience. As the sun rose higher the room became brighter and more pleasant. The underskirts and overskirts and stays and panniers and bodice grew warm under my fingers, the comb drew little shocks from her dry soft hair. Buttons popped, seams strained under my hands, but by and by I learned. When we finished dressing her, she declared herself satisfied with me for the present. And I was well pleased with myself.

"Except your hair, Françoise."

"My hair, Madame?"

"You must learn to dress your own hair properly if you are to dress mine. I must have you looking well."

She took the comb from my hands. Going to a dresser, she opened the top drawer and took out pins and a greenish-brown ribbon that was the same as the trim on my dress. Then she combed out my hair, her hands rough and quick, and bringing me before the mirror again, showed me how to pin it straight back from my face and coil it up behind, and wove the lovely ribbon round it.

When she was done, my thin, straggling hair looked soft. It looked new. When I saw myself in the mirror, I felt that surge of hope. My image made me think I might cross over to what she was, though I could not see how.

"There," she said, when she was finished. "Now you look right, Françoise."

"Thank you, Madame."

She stared at me.

"Are you crying?"

"No, Madame."

She seemed discomfited, and I blinked hard.

"Well, well, go down and fetch my chocolate. It is time."

"Madame?"

"Go down to the kitchen, Françoise. Berthe will have it prepared. I always take some slight refreshment after dressing. You are to bring it to me here."

I got back down to the kitchen with no trouble. It seemed dark and sooty now after the airy brightness of the upper rooms. I hovered near the doorway, peering in. Berthe and the same scrawny kitchen maid I remembered from my interview were preparing a tray that seemed full of little cups and covered dishes, all hot and steaming, with white napkins and biscuits beside. The younger servingman sat at the table also, sharpening a row of gleaming knives.

"Come for the old woman's feed, have you?" he said, tipping back his chair and winking at me again. This time I did not wink back, but stiffened my shoulders. He frowned.

"I am going to take that up to my lady, if that is what you mean," I said, trying to sound as dignified as my new position and remembering what Madame had said about being a proper maid.

"Well, aren't you fine!" he said, raising his eyebrows.

I smiled at the kitchen maid and Berthe, who both stared at me.

"I'm Françoise. You let me in when Madame saw me first. What is your name?"

The kitchen girl smiled and was about to speak when he broke in.

"Don't bother with her, Josette. She's too grand for us, it's plain."

"Perhaps I am too grand for you!" I said, angered by his tone and the set of his mouth. "And you should not speak so of my lady, or I will tell her what you say."

I could see I had gone too far then, for the smile died on Josette's face and Berthe shook her head at me.

"In this kitchen we can say what we like," he said, glaring at me, "and if you carry tales, I will bloody your nose for you."

"You should not speak so to him," said Josette, "and you not here a day yet. Come, tell Paul you are sorry." And Berthe nodded agreement.

"I will not," I said, feeling my cheeks grow warm. "Not when he has threatened to knock me down."

"Suit yourself then," said Paul, and turned his chair so that his back was to me.

I had let my tongue carry me away again, but pride is pride, and not knowing what else to do, I took the tray without another word. I could feel three pairs of disapproving eyes follow me as I pushed open the door and left them.

I paused on the stairs, almost wishing I could go back and say I was sorry and begin again. But remembering the sneer in Paul's voice I pressed on. My service was to Madame

Pommereau, I reminded myself. I would not have much to do with the kitchen or the people in it. I was a proper maid now, to a fine lady, and I should not care to have their good opinion.

When I set down the tray before Madame she stared at it a moment, as if not sure which lid to lift up first.

"May I help, Madame?"

"No, Françoise, this I do myself. Only it is most provoking ..."

She picked up a knife and peered at it.

"What is it, Madame?"

"It is dirty, look."

Following her finger, I saw the faintest smudge on the carved bone handle. Hiding a smile, I nodded.

Sighing, she began to uncover the little dishes, and my mouth watered as I looked on. Chicken sliced thin and mixed with leeks and potatoes, a bowl of white sugar, another of preserved gooseberries, biscuits studded with cranberries, a little jug of cream, raspberry jam, and melted chocolate that poured thickly out of a silver pot into a china cup so thin the light shone through the edges. It seemed to me a feast fit for a wedding, or a funeral. Yet all this gave her no pleasure, it seemed. She picked at the food. Sipping the chocolate, she grimaced and pushed it away.

"Berthe always makes it too strong, no matter how much I instruct her."

If I told this to Marie, I thought to myself, she would never believe it. It had never entered my head that a person could complain of food that lay plentiful before them, prepared so carefully by other hands.

She looked at me curiously.

"What are you thinking, Françoise?"

"Nothing, Madame."

"Really."

"Only … Madame, I have never tasted chocolate before. What does it taste like?"

I sucked my breath in then, sure I had been too forward, but she smiled, pleased again by what she thought was my simplicity.

"Try it then; it is yours. Eat. Drink."

She pushed the whole tray toward me. Glancing at her, I saw she meant it. I picked the cup up gently, fearful that I should break it, and raised it to my mouth. It was sweet and bitter at once, smooth and thick, and like nothing I had ever imagined. I thought she must be a great fool, not to drink it herself. When that was gone I turned my attention to the slices of chicken, and was just spreading a second biscuit with gooseberries when I saw she laughed at me.

"What is it, Madame?" I asked, with my mouth full.

"It is nothing. You amuse me, that is all."

"Why, Madame?" I put the biscuit down.

"You eat so greedily."

"The food is good, Madame. I only do it justice."

"That is not the point, Françoise. It is not well-bred to eat as you do, stuffing it all in at once."

"How does a well-bred person eat, Madame?"

She did not hear the edge in my voice.

"A well-bred person eats small bites, and does not slouch over the table. And most importantly, does not finish the food that is set before her. It looks better to leave something on the plate."

I wiped my mouth and hands on one of the white napkins. I did not want her to think me coarse. If that was what it took to be well-bred, I would do my best to try. Yet underneath, something in my spirit revolted in disgust as I looked at the lovely food that would be wasted.

"Who shall eat it then, Madame?"

"What do you mean?"

"Who shall eat the food that is not finished, Madame?"

"I do not know; it is not my concern. Perhaps the kitchen servants may eat it, or it will do to be fed to the pigs."

She spoke dismissively, already thinking of something else, and I did my best to put the thought away. This was my new life now, and I could not afford to be disgusted by it.

"Françoise. I am sorry I asked if you wept, before. We have both had our losses. But all the same, let us not intrude upon each other, please."

I saw she thought I had wept for my parents. She could not know I wept from happiness, to see myself in full in her mirror at last, to see myself clean and new. She could not have found that a cause for happiness, since it was ordinary to her, and she, it was clear, was not happy herself.

Chapter Nine

That night we sat before the fire in her sitting room. I was too warm, and sweated mightily under the heavy dress, and wished a window open, but she drew shawls about her pale throat as if she felt a draft. She sewed and I did too, though what she worked was a piece of soft white linen while she gave me an old shift to mend the holes in.

I wondered how it was that I sat with her and that her husband did not come to her instead. I wondered if husbands and wives who are gentlemen and ladies do not sit together in the evening, and I wondered where her husband sat, if he sat at the big table I had seen, alone with his papers, pondering the goods he would send to France, counting his money. The men of the fur trade that I had known had all been rough and hard, sharpened by the long winters and the bitterness of their disappointment, coming as they did from France to make their fortunes but making only the fortunes of men like Monsieur Pommereau. As for him, the richness of his house and his wife's refined shivers all spoke of his power, but to me he had seemed small and feeble, not the giant I had imagined such men to be. One of his own voyageurs could have killed him bare-handed in two minutes flat, yet here he was, sitting in his study in his beautiful coat while they sat in their pitiful houses or camped beside their canoes, their faces red with cold.

I thought then of the emptiness at the heart of that great house, with those two sitting alone in it while all around there was bustle and flurry, men polishing boots, women skinning rabbits, and now me too, who would surely work in ways my lady would not see.

I pricked my finger.

"Careful."

"Yes, Madame."

"Françoise," she said slowly, drawing her needle in and out.

"Yes?"

"Yes?" she said, mimicking me, displeased.

"Yes, Madame."

"You asked me this morning about France, and I spoke to you sharply."

"No, Madame."

"I did, because I was intent that you should learn, and it seemed improper."

"Yes, Madame."

"Ask me again what you would like to know of France."

"I do not know where to begin, Madame."

"Then we shall not make conversation, I can see."

I thought of the confused memories my mother had given me of France, and my father too, memories not my own of winding roads and great buildings and cathedrals, of dancing and drinking and music, of the surging crowds and the public hangings and the violence of the people all clashing together. I thought of the pomp of the gentlemen and ladies, glimpsed at a distance or seen through the windows of passing carriages, I thought of my mother stumbling through the streets, or drumming up business outside the theaters.

"In France—did you go to the theater, Madame?"

"No. They have a terrible smell. The crowd, you know, all unwashed and noisy."

I did not know what to say to that.

"But what I remember best, Françoise, is the house of my parents. Where I was born. It was a big house, a white house."

"Was it in Paris, Madame?"

"Oh no. What is it you imagine? I was no great Paris lady. It was in the country, a small village. My mother and father were people of standing. My mother was much taken up with helping the peasant women, with food and clothing and the care of their children. They were most grateful to her. Not like the roughness of people here."

"Madame, there are no peasants here."

She glanced up at me, older, wiser.

"Françoise, do not be ridiculous. There will always be peasants."

She kept looking at me, perhaps thinking that I was her peasant and she would help me to be a proper one.

"When I came here to marry my husband, my mother cried, but I married at her wish, so I don't know why she thought she must cry."

"And were you not married to him before, Madame?"

She did not answer, so I went back to my sewing, trying to make the stitches as small and neat as her own.

"Madame?"

"Yes?"

"Will I do? I mean, am I suitable?"

"Yes, Françoise, you will do very well, I believe, in time."

But there was one more thing to ask.

"Madame, why has your cook no tongue?"

"Berthe? Poor Berthe? Because in France, she told lies. It could have been worse."

"How—worse?"

"Had she been a thief, they might have cut off her hands, if they had a mind to. She came from a small village that did not know the law. It is a shame, but so it goes. And if she had no hands, she could not work and earn her bread. As it is, she can make a good living here instead of starving at home. A woman in her position needs hands more than she needs a tongue."

And then she drew out from the workbasket a pair of black silk gloves. They were thin; they would not keep out the cold. And all along the backs of the hands and up the fingers were designs worked in beads, also black. Jet beads, dull, glossy, not looking like much on their own but all together a marvel, vines and leaves and flowers and yet so simply done, the black against the black, that you had to peer close in to see how fine they really were. A secret marvel they looked in the firelight, though there was a hole in one finger, and a wearing in the thumb of the other.

"Now these I will wear on Sunday next, when I go to church. The blessed Virgin likes to see a well-gloved hand, I have no doubt."

I thought her foolish, then saw she was teasing.

"So you take that one and I'll take this one, Françoise, and I'll show you how to mend it. A glove is one of the marks of a lady. You see, a lady's glove is useless. You can't even make a fist."

She put the gloves on, turned her hand gently, showing me how her hands were suddenly molded, seeming smaller, softer, perfect.

"Perfect," she said, making me jump, "because it is useless. Do you see? It does nothing. It is only beautiful. That is all it needs to be. All it has to do in the world. That is the nature of a glove. They help a lady to remain a lady, even in such a place as this."

She smiled at me.

"This is a valuable pair, but I'm sure you will learn. You learn quickly, Françoise."

I felt a rush of happiness, to hear myself praised.

And so, in the last light from the fire, she took my hand and showed me how to bend the glove, how to mend it.

Chapter Ten

Weeks passed. I knew all the stairs, all the passages, the whole world of the house. I knew how to dress my lady so it pleased her and also pleased her husband, who would glance at her and nod and kiss her forehead before he left her to her sewing each morning. I learned the duties of a maid, and the secrets.

I was a solitary soul in that house, except for my work with my mistress. I had nothing to do with my master or his affairs, and as for the other servants, they now regarded me with suspicion, thinking I might carry tales to my lady. This was my own fault, I knew, but I could not find how to make it right. They had so little to do with me in the ordinary course of things, and so I could not show by my actions that I meant well, and that they had no need to be wary of me. They all had their own work, and their work was mostly below, in the belly of the house. They made the food, they cleaned and polished and ran errands and lived my master's and mistress's humdrum outer lives in their stead, while the Pommereaus in turn occupied themselves with their inner lives and the great work of life, which for my master was the business of the fur trade and for my mistress was her needle and the running of her household and the reading of her Bible.

My master, I found, had no man of his own, though Paul helped him each morning and evening to dress before going away again on all his other work in the house. I was the only one who had nothing to do but wait upon Madame Pommereau. This added to the distance between me and the other servants, who perceived an unfairness in my position. In their eyes, I had nothing to do but dress her and undress her and carry her things. Not many ladies in Montreal had their own maids, being bustling, capable women of the new world who spent as much time in their own kitchens working alongside their cooks as they did sitting by their fires, nodding in the heat.

One evening, I had to run downstairs. I heard them all laughing in front of their kitchen fire, but when I came in the talk ceased, as if I had been Madame Pommereau herself. They were all grouped about the hearth, cracking nuts and throwing the shells into the flames, and very friendly with each other they looked: Berthe grinning all about her; Henri, the other servingman, whittling something of wood; and Josette smiling wanly. Even Paul was merry, splitting open walnuts and digging out the meat with his sharp white teeth. I would have liked to join them, and drink some cider and tell a good tale, as I knew how. But their smiles were private, and not meant for me, and Paul again turned his chair away as he saw me.

"What is it?" asked Josette, rising.

"I need some goose grease, for Madame has a blistered heel."

I smiled, trying to make up, and Josette nearly smiled back, but Paul caught her eye and instead she jutted her chin at the sideboard.

"There it is, in the jar, as you see."

I got the jar and stood irresolutely in the doorway.

"I will not tell on you, you know."

I saw at once I should not have spoken so directly, and had made a mess of it again.

"Who's to say we're saying anything worth telling?" asked Paul.

"I only meant—"

"You should go on upstairs," Henri said gently but firmly, "for she hates to be kept waiting."

I nodded and turned away, not knowing what else to do. As I closed the door behind me I heard Paul say, "It must be easy, having so little work. Who does Madame think she is, to have a maid all to herself and never set foot in the kitchen? She is not in France anymore. And we slave away while that girl does nothing but hand Madame her needlework."

And then a soft chuckle of agreement from Berthe.

"At least I do not sit gossiping before the fire like so many old crows!" I called through the door. And Paul's sharp bark of laughter pursued me up the stairs.

❧ ❧ ❧

It was not as easy as it seemed, and it did not seem, in time, like little work. Madame Pommereau kept me in a whirl. She might always need something else, there might be something that I had forgotten to do, or that I had done ill. I was always trying to please her, always afraid to fail. My work seemed smaller than the time it filled, and yet I was not idle.

I wondered myself, at first, why she needed her own maid when Josette would have done for what she really needed from me, and saved her household the expense and trouble. In time, though, I came to believe she did need me, that a lady must have a maid, and that I was important in being so. And so I came to be of her kind after all, and the other help knew what they were about when they would not welcome me to sit by their fire. Anyway, I sat always with her.

When I was finally, as she said, truly fit to be seen, she took me with her to Sunday Mass. She wore a black dress and I also dressed in black, walking behind her on the way to church. I could dress my own hair now, and hers, and was almost as clean and fussy in my ways as she was herself.

Before this, she had left me every Sunday morning, after I had dressed her. She lent me a Bible and told me to read it. It astonished her that I could read. Her surprise seemed to carry a thought that people of my station could not read, not because no one had taught them, but because they were too simple to be taught at all.

"And," she said to me, though as if she were speaking to someone else, "is it not unkindness, to teach such girls as you to read?"

"How—unkind?"

"Because to read is to imagine another life, a world elsewhere, is that not true? And for a girl, especially a servant girl, to read would surely mean to learn to imagine such another life, and so be dissatisfied with how she must live and what she has been born into. Surely it could only lead to unhappiness, Françoise."

I did not know what she wished me to say, and so did not answer. It seemed that she felt reading would lead to the knowledge of freedom, but not the knowledge of how to be free. And there was nothing to say to that. Yet at her words I felt the same flash of dislike as I had felt about all that uneaten food. But I buried it deep. Besides, I was growing used to her careless patronage and the richness of her meals, and it seemed less strange as time went on. Slowly, I was learning, as she had promised I would.

But I was glad of the Bible she lent me, for my father's Bible I had buried with him. The Bible Madame Pommereau gave me was much handsomer, a dull red-brown stamped with gold. Those weeks before she took me to church with her I had loved reading it alone, not so much for the words, as I knew them well already, but for the feel of the pages, the neatness of the print, the clean smooth covers, and the pleasure of doing something for myself. I dreamed of asking to read the books that lined the shelves of her husband's study. He never read them—they gathered dust—and I thought sometimes as I passed his door of the things he had that he gave no thought to, and how I would love them if they were mine.

I had not been to church since my parents' funeral, and wondered what they would think of me now. I walked slowly and sedately, my steps measured to hers, her shawl bundled in my arms in case she should take cold during the service. In black, I looked again like a mourner, but my coat hung warm about me, and for the first time in my life I saw my breath swirling in the cool fall air but did not feel the wind through my ragged clothes.

The church was cold and drafty and the priest full of such zeal that he spat out of his mouth as he preached, wetly, of the duty to tame the land through trade and commerce and to convert the heathen. I thought to myself that it was hard on the heathen, to suffer conversion from a man who had not even the dignity to keep his mouth dry.

I looked around, swiftly so my lady would not notice. The church was full, and the priest prayed now in Latin with such fervor that his robe seemed to whirl around him. He was like a great bat hovering above us all—women, men, all striving to fit themselves to this land. Even those who were not born in France, who had never seen it, still heard it in the words of their parents, still thought of themselves as travelers in an alien land. Everyone in New France did, I supposed. Except the heathen, of course, who were no doubt wondering what they had done to deserve the burden of these strange, unhappy people.

With the service done, we walked in the churchyard together. The thin sunlight of late October was warm on my face, and all the red and orange and yellow leaves were bright against the blue sky. Impossible to believe, in the clear air, the visions of hell and the devil and the righteous anger and duty the priest seemed to see everywhere he looked. Even the graves, standing in straight rows in the dying brown grass, were softened by the light.

"Françoise, come here. I have something to show you."

I hurried to my lady's side, where she stood before three stones. When I read what was there, I felt chastised for my pleasure in the day and the sun, and did not know what to say.

Hélène Pommereau
1740–1744
Eternal Rest

Isabelle Pommereau
1742–1746
Until We Meet in Heaven

Son, stillborn
1749

"You see, we put nothing under his name," she said at last.

"Why not, Madame?"

"I do not know, for my husband would not tell me."

"I do not mean to intrude, Madame."

"I know, Françoise. It is natural for you to ask. I think it was too much for him, that last loss. He grieved our daughters most keenly, but truly, men want sons. If we are to leave any mark on this place, we must leave children behind, and sons to carry on a name beyond us. He would not have words carved or give the baby a name, but he gave him his own gravestone, so at least he hoped for that much memory. But he does not like to look at the stones with me."

She turned her head to look at her husband, talking in amongst a clump of men by the door of the church.

"Who can blame him, I suppose. He says we must not dwell on the past, that I must mend my spirits. He is right, of course. There is no good in it."

I suddenly remembered my mother, washing the bloody shift for the lady with the stillborn son, and wondered. And I thought of the small grave outside the door of my parents' house.

"Madame ..."

"Yes?"

"A year ago, my mother had a stillborn boy. We buried him in the hard ground. I think often of him."

She squeezed my arm lightly.

"Then you know, a little, what it means. I am glad to have you to look at the stones with me."

"Perhaps you will have more children, Madame."

She frowned, but not angrily.

"I am thirty-five years old, Françoise. And the boy was very hard to bear. I will not have any more children now. So God wills our fate."

She turned away, beckoned me to follow. Her glove flashed in the light.

❊ ❊ ❊

That night, she was talkative. We spoke easily now, often, she taking pleasure in my questions if there were not too many of them, and answering them as she thought proper, and asking me of my life, of which I told what she would think fit to hear. So we were not entirely truthful together, but I think I knew that we were not, while it never occurred to her that her discretion was a kind of untruth, or that I left out what she would not like to know of me.

"Madame, why did you come here?"

"To be married."

"Like the women who travel here hoping for a husband, Madame?"

She rapped my knuckles lightly, thinking I made fun of her.

"Not like the women who venture here alone, those poor creatures. They must be very desperate, to come so far in hope of a husband, and knowing nothing of who they will get. No, I came as an engaged woman. Though we had not met."

"How was that, Madame?"

"The merchants of Montreal also need wives, and some

prefer to take women born in France. Gentlewomen sometimes come by ship to marry men they have not seen, guided by their own parents and friends who know the man, or know of him. I did not choose blindly. I had heard of him by reputation, and I thought a life of service and wifehood to be preferred, as pleasing to God. Which it is."

"Preferred to what, Madame?"

"Preferred to a life lived alone. I was already twenty-one, and had had no offers yet. My mother persuaded me that this was my best course, and an honor for me. And I thought I might be suitable."

She drew the thread in and out, looking intently at her work as if to admire it. A frilled cap, white, embroidered with red and yellow flowers.

"I was not as suitable as I thought. Though I manage, Françoise. This land is a hard place, but I must endure."

I thought of her slippers warming in the morning, her cup of chocolate, the white bread and choice meat she ate every day, her clothes, my hands combing through her hair and worrying over the lines around her eyes as if her face had been my own, and wondered what she would think of my mother and what she had endured. Then I thought of the three gravestones and the son who had no name to take to heaven, and blushed for shame.

"Françoise."

"Madame," I said, not lifting my head from my work.

"What is it like to be born here?"

"I don't know, Madame, as I know nothing else."

"Clever. Tell me about your mother, then. Tell me where you grew up."

"In a terrible hut, Madame! Nothing but the wind to keep me company! Nothing to eat!"

She smiled, thinking I was joking, which I was and was not.

"But my mother was wise, Madame. She is dead but she knew many things. She told me many things that she remembered from when she was in France."

"Tell me about them."

"Well," I said, warming to it now, "she told me all the things that she remembered from her village. She left it, the village, before she came here, she lived in Paris for a time—"

"A seamstress?"

"No, Madame. She told me that if you want to know your future, stick a sprig of yarrow up your nose. If your nose bleeds, you will be married within a year, if not, then never. And that if a man gives a woman a pin or a ribbon or any such thing on Midsummer, he must marry her, even if he does not want to. And if she accepts the gift, she must marry him, there is no going back. And she told me that a black dog crossing your path at dusk means death. And that if you wash your feet at night, you must throw away the water. Otherwise the dead can smell the water and will come in through your keyhole and sit by your fire. And that if you meet your double on the road, you will both instantly cease to exist."

She was laughing now, as I meant her to.

"And Madame, if a woman is condemned to death by hanging, she must say five prayers to the Holy Virgin and bite her tongue until it bleeds, and that will save her life."

"Françoise, if a woman is condemned to death by hanging, she must marry the hangman. That will save her life much better. Or, if there is no hangman at the time of her sentence, she must persuade a man to become the hangman and to marry her, and that will also save her."

"Is that true?"

"It is not foot water or nosebleeds. It is law. Your mother told you lies."

I was startled, and angered by the careless way she called my mother a liar. As if it was her right to, as if I would not care. And though my mother was no saint, I felt a rush of loyalty for her, hearing her honesty so easily dismissed. I could have returned that her own mother had told her the greatest lie, persuading her it was a wise choice to come here and marry a strange man in a strange land. But I kept the thought to myself, knowing she would see her mother and mine in different lights. Breathing deep, I swallowed my pride and went on with the story.

"And when she came here, too, she saw many things, and taught me to beware of the creatures that live in the woods, and to never go off the path."

"Why not off the path?"

"Because then I might stray into the woods, and the devil lives in the woods, Madame."

"The devil is in hell, and the priest knows it. There is nothing like the devil in the woods."

I sucked in my breath, pretending to be shocked.

"Madame, the devil lives in the woods. Do you not know the story of the devil and the voyageurs?"

She smiled then, seeing how I teased her.

"No, I do not."

"Then I will tell you, Madame. Though it is strange you would not know, for perhaps it was your own husband's men that this story tells of."

I could see from her face I was taking a small liberty, but boldly I paused, lowered my voice, and began one of Mathilde's old stories.

"Well, it was getting on toward winter, and these men were deep in the woods one dark night, and they saw the snow was beginning to fall. And they had a long road of many weeks ahead with the pelts carried heavy on their backs, and each man wished in his heart for home, though all were too proud to speak the thought. But the devil can read our thoughts and know us, as surely as God may. So just then, the devil came to them in a clearing of the trees, and the devil was charming and well-spoken, because he was the devil. So the men stayed to hear him speak, though they knew who he was. And the devil said to these men, 'Come, I will make you a bargain. Get in your canoe, load in your furs, right here in this clearing of trees, and by magic I will send you home. You will fly through the air and be set down lightly before morning at the doors of your own houses.' And all the men were astonished, but one had the wit to say to the devil, 'What is our part in the bargain?' And the devil said to the men, 'It is a trifle. You must only promise that you will not speak one word nor make one sound the whole of the journey, for if you do, I will carry you all straight to hell.' Well, the voyageurs thought this over, and talked among themselves, and they agreed that this would not be hard and that they were sick of the lonely winter. So they all got into the canoe and the devil lifted the canoe into the air and they were borne high over the tops of the trees. And each man had to fight inside himself not to cry out in wonder as they flew. But each man was mindful of the devil's due and did not speak one word nor make one sound. So they flew on and on through the cold air, until, down below, each man saw the light of his own home. And each thought of his home, and his warm fire, and his wife, and his bed, and each man cried out in great joy. And the devil swept down in blue flame and sulfur and carried each man straight to hell."

I fell silent, watching her face, then went on.

"And Madame, it is said that on the darkest nights of winter, you may see the ghosts of those same voyageurs, crying out for the lights of home. It is true, I have seen them with my own eyes."

"Home," she said softly, staring into the fire. "Yes, I can see how men might cry out, forgetting everything else, when they wished for home."

I put my hand over hers, moved to pity in spite of myself.

She drew her hand away, shaking off my sympathy.

"Françoise, you cannot have seen such things. Shame on you for telling me lies and thinking me foolish enough to believe them."

"Madame, I do not lie."

I did not know what she meant by lies. I told her stories, as they were told to me. A story was a kind of lie, I knew, but it was not simply a lie. I saw things both ways, as it were, from above and below. Things were true and untrue, and a lie could be forgiven if it was also a good story.

She stood up, putting away her work and going to the doorway.

"It is time for bed," she said, pushing me out.

"Madame—"

"You are a servant, Françoise. Remember that."

And she shut the door in my face.

Chapter Eleven

A thing may fester in the body and bring down the health of the whole, though the whole be sound except for that one thing. And just so, a thing that seems built upon rock may in a moment crumble away.

The next day, I tended Madame, and she was docile, if more apt to be fretful.

"You lace me too tight. Do you wish to cut off my breath?"

"No, Madame."

I loosed her stays.

"No, no, no. That is too loose, now. You will make me not fit to be seen, sagging like an old woman."

I tried again, and she moved this way and that, like a child who cannot be still.

"Is that better, Madame?"

"It will have to do. You are clumsy today."

"Yes, Madame."

"The blue dress with the white lace about the neck, I think, today."

"It is soiled, Madame."

"What?"

"You spilled soup on it."

"So I did, Françoise, I remember. Why has it not yet been washed?"

"Because, Madame, you asked me not to wash it myself but to send it to Madame Auclair, since the lace is so delicate and the dress is silk. And I have not yet done so."

"You ought to have done. I do not keep you to have you sit idle."

I said nothing, for I was not idle, and she knew it. I could see she was ashamed of speaking so, but like most people, her shame made her angry. She sighed as if in great weariness.

"Well, bring me the yellow dress then, that I wore two nights ago. I do not know what my husband will say, to see me twice in the same gown within a week, but it cannot be helped."

I thought her husband would not notice, but knew it was not wise to say so, and so went and got the dress without a word. With exaggerated care, I made her ready, and she, also making the most of it, flinched at any bungling movement or quick flick of a ribbon or a lace.

When the dressing was done, I thought to myself that she looked very handsome, for her annoyance at me had brought some color into her cheeks.

"What do you look at, Françoise?"

"Nothing, Madame. I must watch you if I am to do my work, that is all."

"Bring me my shoes. No, not those, the other ... there, to the right. You will make me stand about all day. Yes, those, then."

I buckled the shoes in silence. She looked down at me from above, and when I was done the buckling, I looked up into her face and then looked pointedly away, fussing with the hem of her skirt.

"You are dull today, Françoise. Can you not find something to say to me?"

"What would you like me to say, Madame?"

"I don't know. Surely you can find something."

But I could not think how to please her, and so we did not speak.

If we had not been as we were, if I had not been her servant, she might even have asked my forgiveness, for calling me a liar and my mother a liar. I wished, as I smoothed her skirt, that she might speak; I would have readily given up my anger, and we could have gone on, happy. But we were as we were, and there was no help for it. I do not know if this was the obstinacy of our tempers, or the places to which we were born. Perhaps both. But fate, of person and of place, is a powerful thing, and so I could not muster a single thing to say. Our silence grew and grew as I smoothed her skirts and then, pinning up her shawl, I pricked her with the pin.

She turned and slapped my fingers. Not hard, but just enough for me to know that what she had said last night was being repeated now another way: Remember that you are a servant.

We looked at each other in the mirror, my face red from shame and surprise, and hers white and determined. "I will sit alone this morning," she said, holding my eyes in the mirror. "I do not need you for the needlework today."

"Where shall I go, Madame?"

"You shall go and help Berthe. You will attend to me later, when I walk out to the market."

I crept down the stairs to the kitchen, and my face burned in the dark corridor. I did not want to be shamed before Berthe and Josette, but there was no help for it.

I pushed open the heavy kitchen door, which was thick enough to keep the smells of cooking from infesting the rest of the house and reminding my master and mistress where their food came from. Berthe and Josette both swung round to face me, their chopping knives suspended in the air. This had become Berthe's habit when I came in, as if to show me I was getting in the way of her work, and Josette copied her, hoping to please. They were a picture, the pair of them— Berthe so large and strong, and Josette even scrawnier than I was, her face white and drawn from her days spent in the warm dark of that big room.

Berthe raised her eyebrows at me, expecting some request, and then tapped her knife on the table impatiently when I said nothing. My stomach felt hard and hollow and I devoutly wished myself anywhere but here.

"Yes? Cat got your tongue?" said Josette, and then blushed, looking at Berthe, who glared at her.

"My mistress does not need me this morning. She says I am to help you in the kitchen."

Berthe chuckled, a low hoarse sound deep in her throat. It was my turn to blush. Neither of them moved to make me welcome. In my embarrassment, I spoke haughtily.

"Come, Berthe, give me a place and do not waste my time."

Berthe nodded slowly, but a smile grew on her face. She knew, I could see, that there had been some fall from grace for me to be suddenly sent down to the kitchen. Her smile was not kind. I think even then, if I had spoken softly and begged pardon for my former speeches, we might have found some way to start anew. But I tingled with hurt pride under their eyes, and it made me stiff and haughty.

"I do not like this work, but I will do it. Make room."

"Do you think I like it?" asked Josette, grudgingly moving aside to make a place for me.

"Perhaps you don't, but it is what you are here to do, which is not the case with me."

"You are no better than us, you know."

"Be that as it may. Give me a knife and show me what to cut."

❀ ❀ ❀

Potatoes, potatoes, potatoes, piled in heaps on the table. Cut open, they oozed raw and wet. My head spun from the heat as we went on, and no matter how many I cut, it seemed Berthe plumped another load down before me. As I worked, I turned my exchange with Madame Pommereau over and over in my head, her imagined voice ringing in my ears. *Remember. Remember that you are a servant. Remember who you are.*

"But I must be more than that!" I said aloud as the knife slipped and nicked my finger. I stuck my finger in my mouth and tasted a thin sliver of blood.

"Don't do that! You'll only make it worse!" cried Josette. "And besides, it is nothing to cry over. Why, my hands are full of such marks. And don't mix your nasty spit up with the food by sucking the cut. Here, wipe your hands and go on."

"I hate this filthy work," I muttered, spitting out blood onto the floor as I rubbed a rag over my finger.

Berthe wheezed disapproval and closed her hands over mine, to show the shape I should cut. My hands had changed, I saw now, from the first day I had come to this house. They were smaller, softer, paler. Not quite a lady's hands, but something nearer to that than to my scabbed capable fingers of a few months before. I hated watching the greenish-gray juice of the potatoes squeezing over my skin.

How was there a way beyond this, I asked myself, watching the piles shrink and tossing the waste scraps into the pig's bucket at my feet. God might decide Madame's fate, but she decided mine. I had imagined, in my ignorance, that I would get beyond myself through her, but she was no way beyond myself. For her to exist at all, I had to remain exactly as and where I was.

The truth of this thought bore down upon me like a blow to the face and I put the knife down, staring again at my softened and pliant hands. It was no good. My hands might look like a lady's hands, but I would always be only a servant, forever. This new life I had found myself in had nothing beyond it, no way up or out. I was a captive, as surely as if I had been scrubbing old sheets back in my mother's kitchen. No matter how friendly Madame Pommereau was, or how open, I would always be her servant and nothing else, and I must remain her servant to have any value in her eyes at all. My position convinced her of her own. And so I was held in place.

In that moment, it seemed I had no home at all, and no hope of one, ever. I did not belong in the world of my lady, and I had kept myself from the world of the kitchen. So now I drifted somewhere in between, trapped and alone.

"But what am I to do?" I whispered.

Josette giggled.

"Berthe, she's loony."

But Berthe peered at me curiously, suspicion in her eyes. I think my face must have gone white.

"You're not going to be sick, are you?" asked Josette, wrinkling her nose.

"No," I said, too loudly, trying to recover my wits, "but don't pry. Just let me be."

"Suit yourself," she said, turning away. Berthe kept her eyes to my face.

"Don't stare at me so! Do you think I'll steal the silver if you aren't watching?"

She raised her eyebrows and I stared at her, unsmiling. Then she heaved a basket of carrots under my nose, and I began to peel.

I was careful to be silent then, but I could feel that Berthe still watched me out of the corner of her eye. Josette, deciding to ignore me, began to rattle on, pausing only to let Berthe make small noises of approval or dissent.

"I'm to go home at Christmas, you know. I must go home, for my sister is to have a baby, her sixth, and I must get home to help name it and to see it christened and everything. I hope it will be a girl, don't you? She has been blessed already with so many boys. Her husband was pleased at first, but now he says the house is too loud and he wants to know who will care for them when they are old. Do you think it will be a girl?"

She asked this with such trust, and Berthe smiled and nodded down to her, and I looked hard at the rough surface of the table, suddenly wishing for Mathilde and some simple kindness. All the fine food I had eaten and the good dress I wore seemed like nothing compared to my loneliness. Berthe patted Josette's shoulder and I blinked with great determination, and kept on with my chopping. As the time passed, my hands grew quicker, and the stinging of my cut lessened, and I regretted bitterly my high-and-mighty speeches. A shrieking, petted thing I must seem to them.

When I was done the carrots, I went and stood before Berthe, looking her in the face.

"I am sorry, Berthe, that I called this filthy work."

She nodded, waiting.

"I should not have spoken so, but my tongue sometimes plays tricks on me."

She looked me up and down, arms folded.

"I will go now, I think. But may we not part well?"

Her eyes were narrowed, trying to read my face. Then she shrugged and turned away without a smile or any sign to show we might end on good terms.

"Well, that is your loss," I said, stamping my foot. And I left them standing in the kitchen and clattered noisily back up the stairs.

❊ ❊ ❊

That night I lay awake in my small room, sorry and angry at once. I slept alone in the attic, the privilege of my position, for Berthe slept in a room off the kitchen with Josette, and the men slept in the back of the house. Mine was a bare room, with a narrow bed and a trunk beside to keep my few things in, along with the clothes Madame had given me to wear. My little mirror was propped on the trunk, my mother's brooch beside it. Above my head were the rafters, shadowy and cobwebbed. No wind blew in, for the roof was snug, but the chill air was stale and dusty. Beetles and mice whispered about in the corners, and I could sometimes hear bigger creatures scrambling about in the darkness outside, rats or squirrels looking for a place to nest. Sometimes owls hooted near the small window, and the stars seemed bright and close. It was rough and unfinished, but I had loved it from the first, because it was mine. Yet now it seemed like a cage. Lying in my bed, I could see nothing but this, stretching on—for how long? Years? A life? In service to my lady until I was withered, comforting her age? What else could there be? What could I be? Where could I go?

My mind stretched through the town, the marketplace, the stone church, the winding cobbled streets and fortified walls, and the bare earth waiting to be made into roads. All the huddled houses, each one a fortress in the dark. Even the shacks where me and mine had lived, even those were a kind of fortress against the dark. And beyond the outer edges of the town—what? More earth, stone ranging along it like a thicket of broken teeth, the trees slowly growing, choking out the air, as they had before we came and would after we were dead. And beyond that, the water that bore the ships from France, and the great ocean full of storms, and France itself, France that had put its boot on the face of this land, France that all New France lay dreaming of. That my mistress dreamed of, in her troubled sleep—her old life there, and all the old orders and ways and customs and positions that continued here, because of that dream of France. I felt it all to be a great weight, bearing down on me, holding me always in place.

I slept badly.

The morning was sour for me. I could think only of how I was locked in my position, and how there was no help for it, and so I began to think of revenge. How or what kind I could not have said. It was like a tickle, or a little pain, this wish. And yet I knew Madame was not my enemy. What I wanted vengeance on was the world she inhabited, the world that kept me always in my place. I wanted a small corner of something that would prove that I was not only her servant.

She felt it in me, this new wish. I would find her looking at me with sadness or confusion, and she would make as if to speak and then change her mind, not knowing what to say. It infuriated me, because she was like a child that has been hurt and cannot fathom why, rather than a grown woman who must consider her actions in the world. Yet there was no outer discord that day, or the next day, or the next. She did not send me to peel any more potatoes.

The real cold of the dying year set in, and at night we sat shivering even with the fire. But rather than the snow we had all expected, rain set in, a cold rain that burned like ice. It rained and rained, the streets ran with mud, and in the graveyard all the sod washed away so on Sunday my lady could not even get close to the graves for fear of sinking her slippers in the mud. The soldiers cursed in the street, slipping like fools, and the officers were in a foul mood, caught from their men, who were sick from the close wet of their quarters, the damp wringing from their sheets, and the food with a fine fur growing over it.

All was not well in my master's work either. He was gone late most nights. With his constant industry and diligence, he was often absent as it was, concerning himself with shipping routes and expansions and patents. I had many times heard him rant to his wife about the treacherous Frenchmen who had gone to work for the English, and how if he had such men in his power he would show them no mercy, and she would nod and smile and say he was right, it was very shocking. But now his upset was so great that it spread throughout the house. There were whispers, whispers in the kitchen that got so loud even I heard them. There was unrest among his own men, and he was troubled. Discipline was slack, there was drinking, angry words. It frightened him. He had never in his life considered that what threatens is not always outside, that discontent or even violence might lie within his own ranks, or in his own house. At times when he spoke I wished he could hear the way even his own servants sometimes talked of him, when they gossiped in corners, not knowing I was near.

"I give them work," he said to Madame one evening when he came to bid her goodnight, "and I give them authority and protection and guidance, I give them all of myself. And I expect loyalty in return. A man must follow his master as he follows God, for what is there to bring us to the knowledge of God but obedience? And commerce itself is a sacred trust, for our business is pleasing to God, and so we may build a prosperous and Godly nation, not a land of squabbling and cutthroat ways. I am here to build the land. And if I am crossed in my task, I must punish them, for otherwise there will be no order at all. But I cannot make them understand this."

And Madame nodded and did not look up. He then looked at me. I also kept my eyes lowered, watching the movement of my hands.

"Even Françoise, in her way, obeys authority. It is simple, what is between women. It is a simple thing, but it is noble also, is it not? She obeys you because you, to her ordinary mind, are an emblem of authority itself. And if she were to disobey, you must punish her. And she, because she is a good girl, would know that the punishment was just. Is that not so, Françoise?" he asked.

And I nodded but did not speak, and Madame and I went on with our work. The needles, in and out, in and out. Then he said he was tired and, kissing his wife's hand, went off to bed. And a little later, she followed him.

Chapter Twelve

The night of my sixteenth birthday, I got up from my bed in the darkness, lit a candle, and crept down the stairs. Every step seemed loud as a pistol shot, and I was skittish as a colt, expecting I would wake the whole house and find myself surrounded by people asking what my business was. But no one stirred. I went slowly, slowly, until I came to the door of my lady's sitting room. The floor was cold under my feet, and the winter air cut through my nightdress. Shivering, I pushed open the door, which mercifully did not squeak under my hands.

In the darkness, the sitting room looked different. I thought of it as a warm and comfortable space, but with the ashes dying in the grate and the moon shining through the window, it seemed eerie and deserted. Even the chairs were unfamiliar, frightening shapes. But I could not lose my courage. I went into her dressing room. The engraving on the wall looked very lively in a shaft of moonlight, and I thought for a moment that the dancing ladies and gentlemen moved, and that the eyes of the king rested on my own. I kept my gaze away from it, for I could feel my fancy getting the better of me, and it was all I could do not to turn tail and scamper back to my room, to hide under the covers till morning. I was almost at the bedroom door now. I could hear from behind it my mistress breathing heavy in her sleep. I brushed the door with my fingertips. My fear left me and I felt a strange exaltation, picturing her sleeping sound, not knowing I stood on the other side. It made me feel she was at my mercy. I did not wish her ill, yet I relished the thought all the same.

I drew out the black gloves from the top drawer, and the jet beads glowed like living things in the light from my candle. The drawer was full of gloves, but this pair was all I wanted.

With the gloves crushed in one hand, I turned and went carefully back to my own room. The stairs seemed even louder and more treacherous, and I trembled, though not with cold. Once I had shut my door, I sat down on the bed with the candle on the trunk beside and drew the gloves on. My hands were like her hands now. As small, as shaped, as delicate. That was all it took.

I lay there a long time before I slept, looking at my transformed hands, thinking that now I would have a secret with myself, something that would save me from her, give me sway over her, if only in my own mind.

Then I put the gloves in the inside pocket of my dress, hung up neatly for the next morning. I could not wear them openly on my hands, but I could wear them on my body, by my skin. Whatever she might think of me, whatever I might be in her eyes and the eyes of the world, something of hers was now mine. And secure in that knowledge, I slept well.

Chapter Thirteen

I had been a fool. It was not possible she would not miss the gloves. I knew it by morning, when it was too late to slip them back into the drawer.

Yet my luck held. That day it turned truly cold. The snow began to fall at last, and we sat at home. The wet streets turned to ice, then the ice was covered in white. We found ourselves snowed in, and while constrained in the house, there was no need for gloves.

"Françoise. Go to the window and tell me what you see."

"I see nothing, Madame. There is only white. I cannot even see the roofs of the other houses."

"Well, well, come back and sit by me then. We must keep indoors today."

And so we sat by the fire. As the days passed, the room grew warm and sleepy. Nodding beside her in the light of the hearth, I slowly felt myself grow warm toward her as well. Perhaps with my theft, I felt the slate wiped clean. And she, feeling the new peace in me, thought order was restored. On the fifth day, when the snow ceased and I dressed her for her walk, I brought her a pair of warm woolen mittens in place of light gloves. She drew them over her hands without thinking, and so we went out.

It was the coldest winter I had ever known, and I thanked my stars as it wore on that I was harbored safe in the Pommereau house, not still in my parents' home. The city was white and still. Even the skyline seemed stretched and brittle in the cold. Everyone huddled by fires, or froze. I heard strange tales of farmers going out to do the milking and being discovered the next day, frozen solid three steps from their own doors; of birds falling like stones out of the sky; of icicles—as long as a tall man—breaking off from the eaves of high buildings and spearing passersby straight down the middle so that they fell dead in the snow.

Winter storms threw great towers of ice up into the harbor, along the beach and against the sides of buildings, so it seemed as though we were under attack from both the water and the air. The fierce wind blew off any snow that settled on these twists and cascades of ice, and my mistress and I went down to the harbor to wonder at these monstrous growths on the frozen sand.

She found I had never learned to skate, and resolved to teach me. Together we tramped out to a large pond used for the purpose and she showed me how to strap the metal runners to my boots, then made me fasten up her own.

"Did you truly never do this as a child, Françoise?"

"I did not have such things, Madame."

"I learned as a child. Every child in the village knew how to skate."

Thinking of my one pair of shoes, I wondered if this was

true. Even in France, surely some children in her village must have been without skates, or shoes, or the warm coat she took as her due.

She smiled at my puzzled expression.

"You will learn. Come, pull me up."

I heaved her onto the ice and staggered after her, slipping and wobbling. But she, though larger and heavier than I, skated right out to the middle of the pond, beckoning for me to follow. On skates, she seemed lighter and more graceful. I could imagine her as a young girl. I tried to follow her, moving inch by inch, never lifting my feet from the ice.

The pond was full of people, all intent on the same sport. Ladies and gentlemen, gliding round and round, some linked arm in arm. The men managed to look more graceful than the women, who were hampered with their wide skirts and bulging shawls and cloaks. All in all I thought it a foolish pastime, to circle endlessly round like a clock. I saw a group of ragged girls standing by the bank. They had no skates, and so they pushed each other across the ice, whirling and laughing. None of them were girls I knew, yet I still wished for a moment to be among them, as ragged and cheerful as they, though their faces were blanched with cold, and their lips and hands terribly roughened by the wind. Lumbering toward Madame, I saw how some of the younger gentlemen skated faster and faster, leaping and capering, and wished to do the same.

"Come quickly to me now. You must be bolder if you are to learn."

I lifted my feet up then, hoping to glide toward her, imagining the wind singing in my ears as I gathered to surprising speed. I slipped and fell flat on the ice in a mess of tangled skirts, my arms waving wildly, my hands clutching air.

"My goodness, are you hurt?"

I stared up at her face, framed in the light from the sun.

"Not at all, Madame, but I think I am not meant to be a skater."

I grinned up at her, and she laughed, and I laughed too, louder than she. Helping me up, she showed me how to lift my feet, how to turn, how to make the blades obey me. By dinnertime, I could keep upright, and even let go of her arm.

"You've done well, Françoise," she said, before she went to bed.

"Have I?"

"It is a sport for ladies, needing a light touch and grace. I like to see you master it. It is a thing that reminds me of home, and I have little to remind me here. Thank you."

It hurt me to be thanked, for it made me think guiltily of the stolen gloves. But I pushed the thought away.

※ ※ ※

At last the spring came. The birds flew among the trees, nest-building, and green things stood up sharp in the wet dark earth. The days grew slowly longer, and the air was sweet in the evening. My mistress seemed to wake more cheerful, and sang sometimes at her sewing. With the warmer weather, she still did not miss the gloves, for she wore a thin gray pair when she went out. And I thought hopefully now that perhaps she never would miss them, with so many pairs spilling out of her dressing-table drawers.

All winter I had kept the gloves against my skin. Sometimes, bending over, I felt the beadwork tickle, felt the scrape of the black silk. Sometimes even, in my guilt, I thought they rustled loud enough for others to hear. Often at night I took them out and wore them, turning my hands in the light of my candle. But with the coming of May, my revenge seemed stale to me. Each day, Madame and I went walking together in the fine weather, and it seemed to me that the world grew larger, and that my theft was not freedom but childish petulance. Whether my servitude felt less, or whether I had grown used to it, I did not know. Yet I still kept the gloves, unsure of how to give them up.

"Françoise, get my cloak and your own," she said one morning, "and good shoes for us both. We are walking far today."

"To visit the churchyard, Madame? We could pick some lilac to lay there."

"No, Françoise, though you are a good girl to say it. I thought today we could walk to your old home."

My mouth must have fallen open, for she raised her eyebrows.

"Is it so shocking? After all your stories, I would like to

see where it is you lived. Could you not take me?"

"Madame, it is not a place for you. And it is too far for you to walk."

"I am strong enough for long walks—as well as you. And do not tell me my place," she said, smiling as she said it, "or I will remind you of yours. Come, this is a new land, and perhaps I should not be so squeamish if I am not to die of boredom."

Then she drew something from her pocket.

"Françoise, you have served me well all winter, and I think I have been a melancholy woman to serve. So I thought, it being spring, you should have something from me."

And she held out to me a lace ribbon, black and red with a pattern of butterflies and daisies woven through it. I kept my palms closed, not knowing what to say and full of confusion, so she took one of my hands and gently forced apart my fingers, and closed them again over the gift.

"I thought to give you this some time ago, but it seemed for a while that we were not friends. So here it is now."

I muttered thanks, my face reddening.

And she smiled so I must smile back. Looking up, I saw she was pleased, thinking my awkwardness a touching humility, when in truth it was guilt. But seeing how she was pleased to think me humble, I felt a little less guilty.

"There, my good girl, tie it up in your hair and get our cloaks and let us go."

In my room, I struggled into my overshoes, and my fingers

seemed heavy. Catching sight of my face in the little mirror, I saw myself white and afraid. The gloves seemed a great load under my dress.

I stood up, and then tugged out the gloves. If we were to be friends, as she had said, I would not carry them with me. Later, while all the house slept, I would put them back in her drawer, and I would make a new beginning in which I might be satisfied with the life I had been given. No one would know of my secret theft, and with time even I would forget it. I smiled at myself in the mirror, touched the new ribbon, and thought I looked like a pretty, obedient, and virtuous girl, and would soon be so.

I left the gloves balled up under my pillow, waiting for night.

❦ ❦ ❦

My parents' house was more crooked than I remembered it. While I did not miss the place, memory had softened it and in my recollection it had not been falling to pieces. The weight of all the winter snow had made the roof cave in on one side, and a soft mossy green had begun to cover over the whole. I imagined, inside, the bed a nest of mice, and the table and chairs slowly turning to sawdust, eaten by woodworm and damp.

The door swung crazily open, hanging by one hinge. We stood in the yard, looking at it.

"Well," she said at last, "is it much changed?"

"No, Madame. It is only older and more bent."

She looked puzzled, and I hid a smile, wondering if she thought I had grown up in a house with only half a roof.

"You must have suffered greatly in winter."

"Yes, Madame."

"And only two rooms!"

"Yes, Madame."

"Well, let us try if the steps are safe."

"We will not go in, Madame."

"Why? Is it dangerous?"

"Dangerous?"

"Might there be thieves living in it, or heathen?"

"There is nothing worth stealing, Madame, and the heathen have their own homes. They do not want ours."

"Then show me."

"Madame, you will think me a peasant, but I would rather be shamed in my superstition than bring on my bad luck."

"Why? Is it cursed?"

She looked round, eyes widening, at the dirt of our yard, the furrows of mud made by the pressure of the now-melted snow, the piles of soaked old garbage, the house itself, and behind that the beginning of the dark trees. It frightened her a little, I could see, frightened and moved her at once.

"When I left this house, Madame, I vowed I would never come here again. I wanted to make another life, and forget my old one. So I closed the door for the last time."

"And yet you came back when I asked you to."

"Because you wished to see it, Madame. I could not refuse, could I? For if it was not for you, I would never have left it."

She nodded, pleased with me, peasant that I was.

"But you will not go in. I understand, Françoise."

She took my arm, as if I were her daughter and not her maid.

"Well then, my dear, enough of this. Lead me home."

❦ ❦ ❦

The market, when we passed by, was in an uproar. There was shouting and the sound of a struggle, and then we saw someone hurried away between two officers, but such a crowd was gathered that we could not see who was held between them.

"What is it, Françoise?" Madame Pommereau said, alarmed. "Run and see."

She hung back in a doorway, and I dashed into the thinning crowd of people, all muttering with disappointment, for the officers had taken their man and gone.

I found myself face to face with Marie.

She was shabby, in a patched dress and with no cloak, though the day was cool. She stepped back from me, looked me up and down. I found myself both proud and embarrassed at the contrast between us, she in her ill-fitting rags and me so neat and clean, with my hair tied with my new ribbon and not a spot on me, from collar to pointed shoes.

"Well, you have done well, haven't you?"

I blushed.

"Not badly. I'm a maid now, to Madame Pommereau. There she stands—there on the edge of the crowd."

"I know it. Everyone knows how you have moved up in the world, to serve in such a house as hers. You are grown greater than us."

I did not know what to say.

"Come, I do not mind. Look at your lovely clothes."

Then she held out her hand. Confused, I made as if to take it, and she laughed, a little scornfully.

"Careful, I might dirty your hands! No, look at my ring."

It was a brass ring, greenish-gold on her finger. It was too loose, and I could see that the metal had stained the skin under it. I wondered if her hands had been plumper when she had first put it on.

"My man is a trapper, we were married before the snow. I'm a married woman now, so you must respect me too, for all your new station."

"It's a fine ring," I said awkwardly.

Then neither of us knew what to say.

"Well, I suppose the mirror did show me something after all!" she said at last, swinging her arms in forced bravado. "I should go now, he'll be angry if I keep him waiting."

"And my lady also," I said. Then we both laughed.

"Well, Marie, we all must serve someone, I suppose."

She stopped laughing.

"I'm married, as is proper. I would not bow to Madame Pommereau for any good clothes. It is not the same service."

"Maybe not. But tell me what the crowd is gathered for, or Madame will scold me so I wish I had your trapper, which I do not now. My mistress thinks it is a rebellion."

Marie wrinkled her nose.

"Ladies and gentlemen are always thinking we may rebel, Marie, and so we might, for if you saw the food I eat every night, you would rebel, and that's just the scraps from their table. Meat and wine and chocolate every day in the Pommereau house."

I saw her eyes kindle with hunger at this, but was not sorry, for I would not be pitied for lacking a brass ring.

"It's nothing like that. Two soldiers fought a duel last week, and they arrested one of them, that's all. I think it is a shame, for he was only a recruit this past fall, and he's handsome too, if a little scrawny."

We looked at each other again.

"Well, I must go."

And she turned and walked into the crowd. I wanted to call something after her, but could not think what.

"Let us walk on, Madame," I said, going back to my lady. "It is only two soldiers who dueled, and they arrested one."

She breathed sharp.

"That will go ill with them then."

"They are soldiers, Madame. May they not fight?"

"In battle they may fight the enemy and kill him, or be killed if that is their fate. But we have too many enemies for our men to kill each other over trifles. And too few men. Surely you would know that a soldier must refuse a duel. Did not your father ever need to defend his honor?"

"Madame, my father had no honor to defend, nor my mother, so it was not a question in our house."

"Françoise, do not speak like that of the dead. They are your parents."

"Well enough, Madame, but let us go, the sky is clouding in."

A gentle rain was beginning to fall as we reached the house. Taking Madame's cloak in the front hall, I saw Paul standing idle in the shadows. Taking off my own cloak, I went to him. He raised his eyebrows at me and smiled curiously. Impatient, I thrust the cloaks at him.

"Paul, take these and lay them before the kitchen fire. I must attend my lady upstairs."

He kept his arms loose at his sides. Feeling foolish, I pressed the bundled cloth against his chest.

"Come, take them, for you keep her waiting."

"Take them yourself. I have business with my lady."

Madame had not followed this, but now, hearing the sharpness in his voice, she came up beside us.

"Paul? What is it?"

He looked at me, still holding the wet cloaks, then looked at Madame and bowed his head, a servile little jerk that showed contempt, though she did not see it. I felt my insides go queasy.

"You must come to Berthe. She's upstairs."

"Upstairs? She knows better than to go upstairs."

"You must forgive us, Madame. We knew we should not have done it, but we had our suspicions, Berthe and I. We had the honor of the household to think of."

"What are you talking about, Paul?"

"So, seeing she was out with you, we took our chance. You will excuse us, Madame, when you see what we have to show you. It is a fearful thing that she has done."

"What do you mean? What who has done?"

"Come this way, my lady."

He led us toward the stairs. My steps felt heavy. I hugged the cloaks to me and walked behind Madame, my eyes on Paul's thin back ahead of us.

"Paul, has Berthe gone into my rooms?"

"Not in your rooms, my lady. Come, you must see with your own eyes."

Up and up we climbed, up the stairs to the attic. As we set foot on those stairs, we all heard a sound from behind the door at the top, a strange, grunting, bellowing sound, a sound of urgency and triumph, but with no words. Hearing it, Madame turned to look back at me, her face troubled. I could not meet her eyes. Let it not be true, I thought, let it not be true, please let it not be true.

Paul led us down the corridor and into my room.

"Come in," he said with a flourish, smirking at me. "Come and see what we found. We were right to be suspicious. Something's not trustworthy about her, I said to myself. And I was right."

Berthe stood by my bed, bellowing. She looked vengeful and dangerous, framed in the gray rain-light that came from my small window. When she saw us, she stopped. She looked at Madame Pommereau, then at Paul, and then, with a grim determination, at me. She opened her hands. They held the black gloves.

She pointed to me, grunting, and hoisted the gloves high to make sure we would all see them and know what they were.

Then, again silence. A question in Madame Pommereau's eyes.

"She found them under the pillow, Madame," said Paul eagerly, "and we knew them for yours, seen them on your hands a hundred times I'm sure. I told you it was a fearful thing."

Berthe gave me a look, then, bending over quick, she spat at my feet.

There were many things I could have done. I had a gift for pathetic tears that had won hearts harder than Madame's. I could have played the innocent, protesting that Berthe, in her coarse jealousy of my place in the household, had herself stolen the gloves and put them in my room. It would have been believable; it could almost have been true. Or, if I had been more noble and thought of Berthe turned out into the street to beg or starve, I could have fallen on my knees and begged Madame's forgiveness, and with my strange luck might even have won it. But when I saw Berthe spit, something broke inside me and everything I was and had made of myself in spite of myself seemed to come crowding up in me and I felt only blind, terrible anger.

I threw myself at Berthe, screaming, my hands clawing at her face.

"How dare you! How dare you! You stupid slatternly cow! I'll tear out your eyes! I'll eat your heart!"

"Paul! Do something!"

At Madame's command, Paul gripped me hard and pulled me off. I still kicked and flailed, pulling at his hair.

"Let me go! I'll kill her! I'll kill you!"

I saw Madame's face and was still.

"Madame—"

She stepped away from me, holding up her hands.

"Don't—don't speak to me. Enough. That's enough. I must speak to my husband. I must consider what to do with you. Oh, Françoise!"

She turned to go.

"Madame—"

"You can have nothing to say to me. Paul, watch her until my husband comes home."

And she went down the stairs.

"Well, my fine miss," said Paul, twisting my arms behind my back, "an example must be made of you."

And Berthe spat again, making a guttural, hoarse sound in her throat.

Chapter Fourteen

"Guard! Guard!"

"What?"

"What is it you read?"

"I cannot read. I am going to light the fire with it, to save us both from freezing to death."

"Let me have it."

"Why?"

"I see my own name upon the paper. Let me have it."

"No. Keep quiet or I'll knock you down."

"Shame on you then. When they send me before the judge, I will complain of my treatment."

He snorted, but thrust the paper through the little grill on my door. I read eagerly.

> We must unhappily report a troubling Incident in the house of M. POMMEREAU, a Merchant who lives within sight of his prosperous Warehouses which employ many in our City. MADAME POMMEREAU, his Lady, discover'd that her Maid, one FRANÇOISE LAURENT, had stolen from her some valuable Items and hid them in her own Quarters. The Theft reveal'd, the Servant LAURENT cursed mightily and threatened Violence to Members

of the Household. Her Vicious Character exposed, the girl was Constrain'd in her Room until she could be taken to some Place more secure. She shall hear her Sentence next week and is now awaiting her Fate. She shall be punished as a warning to all Faithless Servants, and in our opinion, the Punishment cannot be too harsh, for how are we to preserve Order in this new Land, if those who owe us Obedience may at any moment turn on us? Indeed, we will find the Specter of Revolution and Bloodshed at our very Doors if we do not set an Example by which the great Mass of the People shall be held in Check, and through which our sober Judgment and Guidance may Prevail.

In a rage, I tore the paper up, scattering the pieces about the cell.

"Look at the mess you make! Do you wish to be slapped for your temper?"

"It is no matter to me whether you slap me or not. They have me painted as a villain, and I don't know what will happen to me now. Do as you like."

The guard peered at me through the bars, his brow creased with worry and, I hoped, a dawning sympathy. He was an unpleasant-looking fellow, and tired of watching me, but I saw at once a spark of some feeling in him. I slumped down on the bench and put my face in my hands.

"Now, don't take on, don't take on," he said uncertainly. "It cannot be as bad as that."

"It can, though."

Still I did not look up. But I calculated poorly (shivering for days in the drafty basement of the courthouse had made my brain feeble), for when at last I lifted my head, thinking to meet his eyes, he had turned his back on me again and was fussing with the hearth.

"Hey!"

"Will you never be quiet?"

"You cannot hope to start a proper fire by jumbling paper and twigs and logs all together so. It will only smoke but never light, and the paper will be all wasted. You must begin again and build a teepee of sticks all about the paper and the log. The sticks will catch off the paper, and the log from there, if you blow on it right."

He shrugged in irritation, but did as I said all the same and soon had a good fire going. He warmed his hands at it, cracking his knuckles louder than the spitting blaze.

"Thank you."

"New to this, then?"

"We take it in shifts, three days each. I'm a soldier, but only a new recruit, and this is a kind of breaking-in, as it were. I shall go on to other things."

"So I'm your punishment?"

He grinned at me.

"Yes. I was warned you were a trial. Always chattering away or asking for something."

"Well, if I've a reputation to keep up, can I ask you something?"

"Maybe. Don't push your luck."

Then it was my turn to snort.

"I have no luck, as you can see. But I need a favor."

"I don't do favors for free, my dear."

"I don't give away my favors, so don't get your hopes up."

He went red.

"That's not what I meant, you filthy-minded girl."

"Well, say that if it saves your dignity. But here's the favor. Go to the house of Madame Pommereau and tell her I must see her."

"I can't leave you here, it's as good as desertion. They'd make me dig my own grave, then shoot me over my own coffin."

"Then later, when you are relieved. She does not live far from here."

"I know where she lives. It's the biggest house for miles. Do you take me for a simpleton?"

I smiled.

"Take the chance. To help a desperate soul."

"What will you give me if I do?"

I looked down at myself. They had put me in a rough gray smock, without a flounce or ribbon, that scratched me with every move I made. It was like wearing a rough sack. But underneath, in a pocket of my shift, I had concealed my mirror and my mother's pewter brooch. I took both out and weighed them, one in each hand. Which was less dear, I wondered, or had less of myself in it? I thought I had given up my past, but both seemed at that moment to tie me to something, something I had no wish to give up.

"Don't waste your time. I don't want the mirror. It's cracked along the side and the frame is all bent—trash from some fine lady's rubbish heap, and not worth anything now. But show me the brooch."

I held it up before him, and he squinted through the bars, for the cell was murky as a tomb. The brooch looked a little tarnished, but it was still well made, and the petals of the rose caught the glint from the fire.

"Look well, for it's good work, and made in France. You could sell it, or give it to a sweetheart, if any girl would have you."

He held out his hand.

"Give me that and I'll do what I can."

Swallowing hard, I pushed it through the bars. I watched as he held it up, then slipped it into his pocket.

"You'll go then? And tell her I must see her?"

He laughed meanly.

"I won't. It would be a waste of my time, for she'll not come to you no matter what I say, and I can save myself and you the trouble. But thanks for the present."

"But you promised—"

"I said I'd do what I could and I do not break that promise, for there's nothing I can do. You'd better sit here and wait, and say your prayers if you like. I won't risk my neck running useless errands for you. So there."

And he turned away and sat down, stretching his legs out before the now-roaring fire, leaving me to curse and gibber through the bars. He pulled his coat up over his ears, and did not look at me again.

So I went and sat, reflecting that I'd been taken for a fool, and thought about breaking his nose, and in time, in the heat of the fire, I nodded and slept.

※ ※ ※

"Françoise."

Opening one eye, I thought I was dreaming. The fire was nearly out, and the cell and adjoining room were almost in darkness. And, looking down at me from across the room was Madame Pommereau.

"Françoise. Wake up."

"Have they locked you up too?" I said, convinced now that I must be dreaming.

"No. He let me in. I have sat here some time. See, he is asleep," she said lightly. Well, ladies always have their way, I thought, shrugging off sleep and sitting up. I could see the young soldier, now dozing in his chair, his breath wheezing out of him.

Madame Pommereau and I stared at each other, and neither spoke for a time.

"Do they keep you comfortable here?" she said at last, looking away.

"As well as may be expected. They do not starve me."

"That is well."

Again we did not speak. I could not think why she had come, unasked, or what her business was, but I thought, wisely, that I should not venture a guess.

"You wonder what my meaning is in coming here, yes?" she said, as if she read my thoughts.

"How do you know?"

"Françoise. You think yourself hidden, but your face is plain as day."

"Well then. Why do you come?"

"I am not sure I know myself," she answered, moving about uneasily. "At first I thought I must not see you. Indeed, my husband does not know of it. In the first days, when you were still in our house, I was too angry, to think I had treated you as I had, with such kindness, such confidence, and that you would repay me—"

"I am sorry, Madame," I said eagerly, but she made an impatient movement.

"I had been betrayed by you, I thought. For it is true, is it not?"

I made no answer.

"And so, setting the matter before my husband, I knew I did right. And then he seemed to judge with such severity, to see the matter in so grave a light—it seemed to take on a life of its own, beyond anything I had meant."

She kept her head down, and her voice dropped to a whisper.

"And now, these last days, I do not know what to think anymore."

Her voice was nearly gone now. I leaned forward to her, speaking earnestly and quick.

"Then you may end it, Madame."

"End it?"

This seemed not to have occurred to her, but I went on.

"End it, Madame. You may take it back, and forgive me, and they will let me go. That is why you came here, isn't it? For you see I am penitent, and so I am. I will go away and not trouble you, if you do not want my service anymore. But I beg you, let me go. Let me out. Let it end now. It is a little thing that I have done."

She looked up, and I saw my mistake. Her face was troubled and confused, but underneath the confusion I saw anger forming, not forgiveness.

"You do not know of what you speak," she said curtly, "and you think like an ignorant child. I cannot end it now. I have compromised my dignity already by coming to see you at all. I would humiliate myself to end it, and what is worse, humiliate my husband. When something is set in motion, Françoise, it must run its course. Authority, property, law— these are real things, which it is a duty to preserve. And when offended, remedies must be sought, and punishment is now the remedy. Once the process is begun, there is no end, no help for it. You are foolish to think otherwise."

She saw the terror in my face, and looked down at her

own clasped fingers.

"I only wanted, Françoise, to say to you that I wished it could have been otherwise. That I think of you. That is all."

"And I cannot persuade you?"

"No."

I could have tried, all the same, but I was suddenly so weary, as if all my bones had turned to stone inside me. So I simply looked.

"Françoise?"

I made no move.

"Why did you take the gloves?"

"Because, Madame, I wanted to have one thing in this world that was mine."

And her face snapped shut, and she turned to go. I lifted one hand, thinking to catch at her skirt, but thought better of it. She went past me, her long dress rustling along the stones, and shut the door behind her. I was left alone, with the fire nearly out and the shadows reaching for me.

Chapter Fifteen

At trial, my mistress gave evidence against me, as did Paul, speaking both for himself and for Berthe. Frustrated by her lack of words, Berthe herself would not be quiet during the proceedings and was sent outside, where her noises troubled no one.

I looked hard at my lady, but she never looked at me. Perhaps she thought herself done with me, and now wished only to forget she had ever known me.

Flies buzzed about the courtroom, from somewhere high above us. Even though the weather outside was warm and sweet, the air was cold. I wondered that the flies could survive it.

My master wore his best coat that he wore only to church. As I stared at Madame Pommereau, I wondered who would dress her now. She looked disheveled, indeed, with her cloak on crooked and her skirts not as smooth as they should be. I felt a familiar twitch in my fingers, seeing how poorly she looked, as my hands remembered the actions of fixing and petting, of making her neat enough to face the world.

"Becoming acquainted with the treachery of my maid, I swiftly moved to set justice in motion…"

I saw her husband nod his head to her, as if to steady

or comfort her as she undertook this unpleasant task. He looked tired and irritated. I wondered what important business I was keeping him from.

Her face was white and drawn, her eyes red. One loop of hair wobbled, threatening to come down about her ears. Had Josette dressed her, sausage-fingered, pulled up from the kitchen shaking like a leaf at the terror of the task? I could have dressed her better in my sleep.

As for me, I still wore the rough gray smock they had put me in, and my hair was pinned severely back from my face. As I waited for my sentence I thought, confusedly, that they could not transport me to a colony for my punishment, for I was there already, and wondered if they would send me back to France. Perhaps, when they let me out of prison, I would go and be a whore, like my mother, as there would be no other thing for me to do.

The judge rose, clucking his tongue like an old, fussy woman. He was a thin puppet of a man, despite the authority he held, with a glistening drop at the end of his nose, and furry moles on his face. He peered at me with little pinprick eyes.

"I believe that the picture we have been given of the character of the accused shows strong marks of an incurably bad and wanton nature, given to violence, deviousness, and a total want of the respect, loyalty, and obedience which should be proper to her. While I regret the severity of what I must pronounce, I believe it my duty as a representative of the Sovereign Council of New France to make an example of her, so we will not see further instances of such disregard for authority and property."

He snapped his jaw shut and sat, nodding to his clerk. The clerk rose and read.

"Françoise Laurent, you are hereby sentenced to death by hanging, which sentence to be carried out in the month of December, in the city of Montreal, in the year of our Lord 1751. May God have mercy upon your soul."

The judge waved a hand.

"Take her to prison. She will stay there until her sentence is to be carried out, and it is my hope she will there find penitence and salvation before the end."

As I was led away I heard someone weeping, crying out *please please please*, but as the weeping sound grew louder I realized it was my own voice I heard.

※ ※ ※

They took me to the prison in a cart, my hands tied behind my back. I felt the warmth of the sun and thought this would be the last time I would feel it before they took me out again for the last ride of my life, a ride that would end with a wild jump into emptiness. As I was led into the prison I kept my eyes fixed upon the sun, keeping it in view until the last moment, when the door shut behind me and the warden led me blind along the corridor, my head swimming, my eyes dancing with explosions of green and purple and gold.

The warden ducked my head down with his hand as we went into the cell, to keep me from striking it against the low stone archway, but I stumbled and fell onto my knees. I crawled forward, tried to turn around in the doorway, groveling. I thought if I could only see this man's face, if he could see my face before shutting the door, he would see it was all a mistake. He would take me to my lady and I would find myself again by her fire, sewing, the gloves in their proper place in the drawer, me in my proper place, everything in its proper place.

But the warden kept his eyes down, and when I tried to grab at his boot he stepped back, muttering, "There now, there now, enough now."

I made another grab at him and he kicked me hard. He knocked the wind out of me and I fell back and my head spun and I let myself fall back on the stones and I let my own eyes close and I heard the slam of the door and then the fading sound of his footsteps as he walked away.

The cell was dark and small, with one slit of window. There was a pallet of yellowish-black straw in one corner, smelling of mold, with a rough blanket thrown across it. A runnel of water ran down the wall and gathered in a little pool in one corner, and the stones felt damp and slippery under my hands. Moss grew soft and green in the cracks, and all was dim, with only the one shaft of light from high above my head. I felt as a fox must feel when the trap closes on his foreleg deep in the woods, leaving him to squeal and gnaw until the trapper comes.

Getting my breath back, I screamed into the stones, rolling over and over. I felt something hard in my pocket, and took out my little mirror, the only thing they had let me keep.

There I was: Françoise Laurent, thief, criminal, condemned.

With all my strength I threw the mirror against the stone wall, and it smashed.

Chapter Sixteen

For a long time, there was nothing to do but wait. I sat quiet, my head bowed, and in this quiet I found myself thinking of Madame Pommereau. What had she meant in coming to see me? What had she wanted, what had she thought? What had she expected me to say or do? I also wondered if she knew, then, what might be done to me. Even in my anger and despair, I hoped she had not known, that my sentence had been much more than she had ever intended to inflict on me. For what had I done, that she should hate me so? I knew she did not hate me, indeed I believed she loved me at times almost as a daughter, and that was what made her feel I had betrayed her. And underneath that lay another mystery: the mystery of myself. For I was no fool, and yet I took the gloves, and I wondered, turning it over and over in my mind, if I had somehow willed my own end. If I had taken the gloves not only from my rebellious spirit but from something much darker, something in me that must perversely throw away the good fortune that life had offered me, something in me that must throw away life itself. And this thought was so big and so terrible that I pushed it away. Yet here I was, caught in the hard stone.

The space was small, but I made it smaller still. I sat in

the center of that cell and drew my arms and legs in close to me, huddling in my skirts. I thought to hold myself together that way. The light moved across the floor from the window, high above my head, but it was not enough to fight the darkness. And I let myself be made of nothing but fear. I did not move even to eat or drink. I thought that if I were as still as the stones then somehow fate would not notice me. I would be safe in my little space, and time would not move. Time could not move, because time was taking me closer and closer to the drop.

On the third day the warden did not leave the food and go away again, but came and sat beside me, holding the plate. There was bread on it—I could smell it—and porridge, and beside that a cup of water. But I would not turn to look. He held the spoon up to my mouth but I clamped my jaw tight, and at last he put down the bowl and forced me, gently, to turn my head. I saw him better so close. His beard was beginning to go gray, his face much lined, with broken red veins along the nose, and rheumy blue eyes, kind eyes.

"I've a girl at home the same age as you. I won't say she wouldn't do the same, my daughter, given the temptation. And I think it's a great shame."

I did not answer him, but I did not look away.

"So I won't have you starving, not while I work here."

And he tried again, holding my head like I was a child, maybe his child, and finally he got a few spoonfuls down, and some water.

·"Now that's enough, or you'll spew all over yourself. But I'll leave it here. You eat it slowly today—you make yourself eat slowly."

"And what if I don't eat?" I asked in a ragged whisper, for I had not spoken since they put me in the cell and my voice was hoarse and strange in my ears.

"Well then, you'll die, won't you?"

"I'll die anyway."

"So will we all," he said, getting up and standing over me, "but not for some while. And you won't die just yet, my girl. Didn't you know? There's no hangman in New France to hang you. He's died. Sudden. Fever and drink, damn him. No one to take his place either, for he'd been at his post for years. I thought he'd live forever. And a hangman is a difficult thing to find. No, don't look so hopeful—they'll find one, there's men enough without any conscience, and men enough who need work. But even with all that, it takes some time to find a man. Not many want to do it, put nooses around necks. It's shameful, and those who do it answer to God on the last day, whatever the will of the king or the archbishop or the governor or that Pommereau bitch and her fine husband. So until then, you can keep on living."

"But in here."

"Yes, in here. I can't let you out, my girl. I have children of my own, and a wife too. We each have to make our way in the world. But you'll be alive still. Isn't that enough?"

I did not answer.

"So think on that, my girl, and be content."

And he left me and locked the door behind him.

I got up and ran my hands over that door. It was solid oak, stained dark; it would have withstood axes. It was rough under my hands. I leaned my forehead against the wood, which was cool and swollen with damp. I felt as though I would fall to the floor, but managed to stay upright. Alive. Alive. No one to hang me. Yet. I had time, but time was all I had. Still, better than counting the days and knowing their number.

I slowly ate all the bread and drank the water, and finished the cooling porridge.

❧ ❧ ❧

Drip, drip, drip of water on the stones. I measured my days and weeks by the opening of the door and the face of the warden, my bowl of food. When the door opened, there would be a quick glimpse of the corridor and I would imagine running along it through another door, and another, and then to the world outside. It would be summer there now. The marketplace would be full of good things to eat, the soldiers marching, the ladies walking together, and the men of business hurrying along their way, important, unaware of the bright day, lost in their own concerns, as I had been. I wondered if Madame Pommereau also went to market, if she had a new maid yet, if she ever thought of me.

I did not mark the morning or the evening, but let the hours flow over me. I drifted in a haze of unformed thoughts until I was not certain that any of my life before was real or a story I was telling, or why I was in these four walls. And then I would put my hands to the cold stone and know who I was and where, for the cold went all through me, and there was no escape.

One night I woke, having slept all day. The darkness pressed upon me and I began to sing to myself, hoping it might make the darkness seem less complete.

Oh, the pleasure of love is fleeting,
But the sorrow of love lasts.

My voice sounded so weak and wobbling then that I began to weep, softly at first, and then I sobbed, gasping air, as the sheer loneliness of my position forced itself upon me. Spent, I curled myself up on the stones, my eyes swollen, hoping at least that I might sleep.

And then I heard it. It was so faint I thought it was the scurry of a mouse, the rustle of a beetle, but it went on, from the next cell, the cell I thought was empty, on the other side of the stone wall. Breath. A choked breath, as of someone hoping they would not be heard, too frightened of the darkness to make a sound. I listened. It went on. Then I began to tap my fingernails on the stone. Three taps. I waited, then tapped again. This time, four taps. Silence.

Perhaps I had frightened the breath away. I tapped again, six strong taps. A pause, and then, a miracle. Three little taps against my ear, from the other side of the wall.

And then, behind the wall, a voice. A small, stifled, young voice, as if I had willed it up out of my own terrible need.

"Who's there?"

And I said, "Me."

Chapter Seventeen

"Who's there?" the voice said again.

I crouched down, seeking the place the voice came from. Feeling with my hands, I came upon a little hole in the stones, so small I could not fit the tip of my finger into it, but still, a hole. A cold draft came from it, and I shivered.

What if this was a spirit, something that haunted the cell, come to speak to me? I thought of all the suffering and guilt such a place must hold, that if any place were home to restless spirits, it would be this. I thought of bony fingers meeting mine, of hands without substance reaching out for me in the dark. I wondered also if I had imagined this voice, or if I was going mad. And yet I could not draw back. In my loneliness, I would almost have preferred a spirit to no voice at all, but still, in my sudden fear, I could not speak.

So there was only silence, broken by little scratching sounds from the hole. I could not make my tongue move in my mouth, but gathering courage I began again to tap upon the wall, and in this manner I and whatever it was made noises back and forth, sometimes growing, sometimes sinking to almost nothing.

"Who's there?" said the voice again at last. I could not tell if it was a man or a woman who spoke.

Silence.

"You're not …"

And the voice broke off again.

"What?" I said, whispering.

"Are you …"

"What?" I raised my voice bravely, and I could hear whatever it was scuttle back a little from the hole.

"You're not a ghost?"

I sighed with relief, for ghosts are not afraid of ghosts.

"No. I thought you were."

"I've been listening to you."

The tone was so hollow and sad, with such a breathy melancholy in it, that I became fearful again, still not sure that it was of this earth.

"Are you certain you're not a ghost?"

"I'm not if you're not."

I smiled at that, for the voice sounded friendly now, and almost teasing.

"Well, if you aren't a ghost, then who are you? You whisper so low, I can barely hear you."

No answer. Had I frightened the voice away by being too bold?

"Well, better not answer me then," I said. "It's wise to not tell our names yet. For all you know, I might be the devil himself."

"Not you!" said the voice, louder now. "You're only a girl. I can hear that much."

There was such an easy scorn in this that all fear in me was forced out by annoyance.

"And I suppose you are only a boy."

"I'm a soldier. So there!"

"Well, you aren't a soldier now, are you? You're a prisoner, just as I am."

"But I will be a soldier again. What are you?"

I did not want to answer that. What could I say? Thief? Traitor? Worse than nothing?

"I'm nobody."

"You cannot be nobody, or you could not speak to me."

"Well then, let us say I don't wish to tell you my name yet, and I cannot say something impressive, like soldier. So I think it best to say nothing."

"Fair enough."

I could tell this pleased him, and wondered that he did not notice the slight mockery in my voice. Perhaps he was simple in the head. I leaned forward.

"What did you mean when you said you listened to me? How long have you been here?"

"Well, I have been in the prison some time, but they have only just moved me to this cell. I was going mad from loneliness in the last place. And here I was, alone again. But then I heard you. I heard you singing. And then I heard you crying."

"You did not!" I said, feeling my face grow warm.

"I did. You sobbed like a child."

"You would too, if …"

"If what?"

But I did not answer.

"Why are you here, then?" he asked.

"You first."

"It is very horrible."

"Tell me and I will judge that for myself, my lad."

"Do not say 'my lad' in that way. You must show me respect."

I laughed. I could tell by the way he breathed in sharp that I had angered him now, and his words came out in a rush.

"I killed a man in a duel."

"Is that all?"

I was impressed, really, but I kept my voice cool. I would not make myself meek and worshipful just because he was a soldier, however much he wished for it.

"What do you mean, all? It is a fearful thing."

I relented, leaning forward to the hole.

"Tell me then."

"He insulted my honor as we played at cards one night, so I challenged him, and we met in the woods at dawn, with our friends all about to witness. I sliced him from throat to belt buckle, and his guts spilled out in the snow, but I wasn't sorry. He was a cruel man, and a liar."

"Was he a fierce fighter, though?"

"Very fierce, and twice my size, but I split him down the middle."

"You're scarcely cut from your mother's apron strings, by the sound of you. A shaking scared one, and no older than I am."

"I'm older than I sound, and a master with my sword!"

"And a cat on your feet, and death to your enemies, and all of that, I'm sure."

I heard him shift his weight on the other side of the wall.

"If you could see me, you'd fear me. If you angered me I'd knock you down before you could get a good look in my eyes— if you were a man, that is. I'd be ashamed to fight a girl, for they are too frail for an honest fight. But I am a terror. They had to lock me in here to keep me from more vengeance."

Well then. I could play at this boasting game too. Besides, I was piqued at the thought that I could not scrap as well as he, being a girl.

"Don't be so sure, my fine soldier. You don't know yet what it is I've done."

He drew in his breath. "What?"

I had no fear of his voice now. I put my mouth right against the chink in the stones. I felt again the draft of cold air from his cell, clammy on my tongue.

"If you have been here a long time," I whispered, "then you will not have heard of the gruesome fate of the Pommereau household."

I paused, waiting.

"What? What?"

He sounded eager, and I was sure he had his ear pressed to the wall so I might speak into it.

"I was the maid to Madame Pommereau, who I am sure you have heard of, for her husband is a great man in the fur trade, and the English of the Hudson's Bay Company utter heretical oaths when his name is mentioned. They lived in a stone house with more rooms than you could count. And I was happy to be a servant to Madame, until she angered me by calling me a peasant. I might have been her maid, but I am no one's peasant. And I resolved that she must pay for this. So I snuck out of my bed one night and took the kitchen knife and slit her throat from ear to ear as she lay snoring in her bed. But I did not like to be found out for my crime, so I took care that there was none left to find me. And in my frenzy I killed all who were in the house, starting with her husband, then all the servingmen and maids. Even the old bitch of a cook with no tongue—I slit her throat as well and let her bleed out onto her own draining board, for she had offered me much unkindness and I never forget a slight. So watch yourself!"

I raised my voice at this and had the satisfaction of hearing him jump. Then I dropped back to the barest whisper.

"When all my violence was spent, I took a sack and stuffed it with gold and my lady's necklaces—I even took the rings off her dead fingers—and I fled in the night. I meant to go and live in the woods and answer to no one, and dress myself in skins and eat berries and so go on to some place where my crime would not be known. But the soldiers came and found out where I was hid and took me back, and so here

I am. I'm the monster of Montreal and the terror of New France. News of my infamy will travel over the ocean and the ballad-makers in France will write songs of me and sell them in the street. So tell me, what do you think of me now?"

I heard him breathe in deeply, as though he had held his breath through all of my made-up tale.

"Was she unkind, your mistress?"

His voice had changed. He sounded small, uncertain. I wished to scare him, but now that I had, I found myself regretting it. If we could make friends, I would have someone to keep me company, and I had frightened him away before we had even begun.

"She did not beat me, if that is what you mean."

When he spoke again, his voice was fainter. He had moved away from the hole.

"It is a cruel thing, to do as you did. They had not harmed you. Mine was a debt of honor, and that is a different matter."

He was right, too. My stories had run away with me again.

"Are you still there?"

"I will not speak to you."

"Please."

"It would be below me to speak to you."

"A liar, and a disgraced soldier, sitting on the wet stones. Below you, to speak to me? Who else is there for you to speak to, in this dark place?"

I could hear him shuffling, unsure.

"Come," I said, in a softened tone, "I am not as monstrous as I have told you. No one will make any ballads for me, in the old France or the new one. Speak to me, then, for there is no one else, for you or me, and if you don't speak to me, we'll both sit lonely in the dark."

"I won't."

Losing my temper, I yelled as loud as I could.

"Then Christ's wounds, I hope you rot! I hope they keep you here forever, and no one speaks to you again!"

I kicked hard against the wall, and he kicked back, angry in turn.

"Go away! Leave me alone!"

"I can't go away, you idiot! I'm a prisoner, the same as you!"

Then we both heard steps, heavy boots striding down the corridor. And we both dropped down in our corners, still as mice. I could hear the soldier rustling, then nothing.

"There now!"

It was the warden's voice, outside our cells.

"All right, quiet, both of you. Do you not know it is the middle of the night? You should be praying to God for your sins, not fighting like two urchins over a crust of bread!"

"How am I to know it is the middle of the night," I called to him through my door, "when there is but little to tell night from day?"

This was not even true, as I could see moonlight from the window, but to my satisfaction I heard a laugh on the other side of the wall.

"If there is more shouting, I'll move you away to a farther cell, my girl, where you cannot speak to trouble me. Christ, I hoped to have less trouble moving you side by side, to save myself the walk, but perhaps I was mistaken. Now settle, both of you, and look to your souls."

And we heard his footsteps fading as he went.

I heard a soft chuckle again. Slowly, slowly, I crept back to the chink in the stones, and waited, thinking it best if he spoke first.

Straining my ears, I heard him move toward the hole. We both sat there awhile, neither saying anything.

"Are you there?"

I leaned forward, glad he had spoken first.

"Of course I'm here."

He laughed again.

"You spoke boldly to the warden. It was well done."

"He should not tell me to mind my prayers. Does he think himself a priest, to counsel me?"

"He is an ass."

"No, he is not. He was kind to me, when I first came. But I do not care what he thinks of me, all the same."

"You do not care much what anyone thinks of you, I think."

Was this true? He meant it as praise, but hearing it said so, I thought suddenly that I had no one in the world now whom I cared to please, and this thought made me sad. I did not answer him, and he went on, his voice halting now, and almost shy.

"I get frightened sometimes, of the dark. It would be a comfort to know there was a voice on the other side of the wall. It would make the darkness not so great."

"Yes."

"I would not wish for the warden to take you to another cell."

"I do not wish to be taken. So let us mind our tongues when we speak to him, and not kick any more walls."

"Yes."

"You do not mind that I am the monster of Montreal?"

"I think I have no choice," he said. "Perhaps what you have done does not matter so much, in this place."

I leaned in toward the hole.

"Tell me your name."

"My name is Jean Corolère."

"Well, Jean Corolère, let me tell you something true."

"What?"

I let my voice drop to the sweetest, softest whisper.

"My name is Françoise Laurent, and I was servant to Madame Pommereau. But all I did was steal a pair of her old gloves."

In the pause after I spoke, even with the dark, even though I had no idea what he looked like, I knew he smiled.

"Well, Françoise Laurent, you are a liar, but I am glad you lie."

"Did you believe me?"

"Not really."

He had believed me heart and soul, but I let it pass.

"If I am not a murderer, may we sometimes speak, and keep each other company then?" I said.

"Until the end, we may. I am here some months yet."

"Well, until you go then."

"Will I go before you? How long are you here?"

I pressed my hands against the cool stone on either side of the hole.

"I am here forever, Jean. As soon as they can find a hangman, I will hang."

Chapter Eighteen

Later, Jean slept. I did not. With my fingers, I traced the shape of the hole and thought about the voice behind it.

The hole was small, barely a crack in the stones, low down to the floor. I could have run my fingers along it and not noticed, and yet now it could bring me comfort in this darkness.

I rolled away and onto my back, shifting in the patches of damp straw. High above my head, the thin slit of window still showed moon. I held my hands up, and was just able to make out their shape in the faint light.

A voice in the dark. A voice as lost as my own. Whoever was behind that wall could be shifted to my purposes, if I willed it. He had only my voice to follow. He could not tell if I told lies or truth.

He said he had killed a man. Did I believe him? His voice seemed so slight, so faint. And yet men do kill each other sometimes, in cold and calculated ways. That is what a soldier does. I wondered if I feared him. I had known men who seemed weak and gentle, and yet could be terrible in their anger. The fiercest soldier in my father's regiment had seemed a lisping slip of a thing, but no one crossed him, having seen him in a rage, for he had neither sense nor mercy when pushed too far. Perhaps this boy was such a one.

A voice in the dark—someone to talk to, someone to tell my story to before I died. Because death was to be the end of it, one time or another. So, thinking the matter over carefully, I saw I had no need to fear him, or anything ever again, because I knew the end.

Suddenly I sat straight up, Madame Pommereau's voice in my head.

A woman who is condemned to death by hanging may escape death by marrying the hangman, or, if there is no hangman, by persuading a man to become the hangman and marry her.

And this, together with the warden's voice saying, "You'll not die yet, my girl," and the vacant hangman's post.

I paced the floor of my cell, my hands shaking, my feet rustling the straw and here and there grinding on a fragment of broken mirror. If I could make this voice, this soldier, this boy no older than myself, become the hangman and marry me, then I would live. I had thought so long to stay here in my cell until they took me out to die that the possibility of my life given back almost choked me. I steadied myself against the wall, pressing my forehead against the stones. I found I had tears in my eyes, and yet also that I was laughing.

Letting myself slump down to sitting, I hugged my knees against my chest, rocking back and forth. It seemed so easy. I would persuade him to marry me and be the hangman, and they would let me out. I would escape, far from anywhere my mistress or anyone else could find me. I would be free.

Yet married to the hangman. Not only to the hangman, but to a stranger. Was he fearsome, violent, a monstrous creature? Was he timid, afraid of the world, afraid to live? Would he be kind? I saw myself, twenty years from now, in some grim life somewhere, worse even than my mother's, thinking with longing of the rope that I had missed.

No. Whatever happened, whatever he was, it was better to live. I knew that much.

Yet how could I persuade? I had nothing but my voice to convince him that I was what he wanted, that I could be the life he wanted. And I would have to convince him that it was worth giving up his occupation, his sword, his honor, to have me. I must make him trade in his soldier's jacket for a mask and a noose, a life reviled and disgraced, for no one is lower than the hangman.

The difficulty of it broke in on me then: I must make this stranger love me, and need me, and I had no way at all of doing it save through words. In his shoes, I would not take such an offer. Yet that was my task.

Words. Words could do much. I knew this. I must have faith in this. When there is only one hope left, when there is only one way out, it does no good to think anything impossible.

I buried my face in the straw and shut my eyes. I must be ready for the morning.

When I slept at last, I dreamed of rope, of keys, and of open doors.

Chapter Nineteen

"Françoise? Françoise? Are you awake?"

I shifted, groaned, rolled over.

"Françoise?"

Then I was wide awake, sitting up, watching the hole.

"Françoise?"

"Yes?" I hissed, parched suddenly with thirst and a strange shyness.

"How … are you well?" he asked, his voice also shy.

I crouched down to the hole.

"Well, considering I sleep on the wet straw and stones and have had nothing to eat but dry bread and lumpy porridge for as long as I care to remember, and that I've nothing but the end of a rope to look forward to, I am very well."

Then I laughed, and after an astonished moment, he laughed too, and the laugh seemed to make him easy with me.

"Did you eat better before?" he asked, still laughing.

"At my lady's house, far better. They would turn up their noses at anything that was not fine."

"Tell me."

"Roast lamb and goose and chickens every day of the week. I think they never really thought that others do not eat so well. Though my mistress told me once that trappers eat beavers in the wild, and that the bishop has declared that beaver may count as a fish, so they will not sin on Fridays. It must be a tough, strange kind of fish. So I learned soft ways there, and this has been hard going."

"I am used to food like this," he said, "for it is how soldiers are fed."

"What, only porridge?"

"Slop! Or sometimes, if we are lucky, some meat on stale bread, and the meat cold and near raw, yet we're so hungry we eat the greasy stuff at a gulp and fight over the scraps. While the officers lounge in their rooms with velvet curtains and sip Spanish port out of crystal glasses."

"It sounds a terrible life, beyond enduring," I said, knowing that was what he wished I would say.

"It is. But it is the life of a soldier. It's meant to be hard, but we bear it," he said with great pride.

"And yet how could you fight, hungry all the time?"

"It gives the men an edge," he said wisely. "It makes them angry and quick, if they are a little hungry. It makes them fit for battle."

"It would make me fit to slit my commander's throat some starless night, for the unfairness of it."

"That is because you are not a soldier, and cannot understand obedience. We must obey, or there would be no order at all, and we could not subdue this land."

I heard in his voice another voice, and knew he repeated what someone had said to him, a man like my master, puffed up in his fur-lined coat.

"And it is an honor," he went on, "our hardship is also our honor. Girls don't know about things like that."

Then he sighed.

"And yet I was very hungry and cold some nights, it's true. All those who were unmarried slept in hammocks slung in rows and I would lie awake and listen to the other men snoring and my blanket was so thin and all I could think of was the food my father used to sell."

I thought of rows of men lying in the dark.

I tried to picture Jean in my mind, and of course could not.

"What did your father sell?"

"He had a vegetable barrow in the market, for he was a farmer, though he did not do as well as he had hoped. He did not have enough sons to help him. But we managed, he and I and my sisters and my mother. We kept chickens too, and sold those in the fall, and the eggs all year as well. I used to help him sell, and kept an eye out for thieves. I have a scar on my hand to show for it. My father was ashamed of the barrow and our poor farm. He used to say I would better myself and rise very high in this land. And I have, or I did, till now."

Steady now, I thought, steady. Don't give anything away.

"Now I am a disgrace. But when they let me out, I shall be a soldier again. I will fight bravely, and clear my name. And my father would have no need to be shamed, were he still living. He died last summer—he fell down dead in the field all of a sudden—so at least he cannot see me here."

Red hair, I thought. Red hair and a feckless look, singing to himself. A raw recruit, tripping over his own feet.

"Françoise? Are you there?"

"Of course I'm here. Where would I go?"

"Why are you laughing?"

"No reason. I just thought of something, that's all."

Careful, go easy, go slowly, I thought. I'll get you, my fine lad.

❧ ❧ ❧

We fell into a kind of order with each other as the days went on. It was a lilting, unsure game we played, speaking through that hole. I could feel the more we talked, the more he felt he knew me. He told me much, each day a little more. I told him less, feeding him scraps piece by piece. For I knew enough to understand that my mystery was my strength. The more he had to guess, the more magic I had for him. If I could keep him guessing, he would always wish for more. I spun out the life of the Pommereau house—my master and mistress, the other servants, even the theft of the gloves. I told him tales from before that, of my parents, taking care to make them seem both more dreadful and more pathetic than they had been in life, to awaken both his sympathy and his admiration without asking for it in words. Yet though I told him stories of the lives surrounding mine, I managed to avoid showing too much of myself, so I remained a dark spot in his vision of me.

"What do you look like?" he asked me one day.

"Why do you want to know?"

"No reason," he said, and I heard the blush in his voice.

"Tell me what you think I look like."

"I … I have no idea."

"Well then."

"Well what?"

"Well then, tell me why you want to know."

"Because I wish to know, so I do not always wonder."

I considered this, pondering how much to weigh out.

"I have very black hair."

"Yes?"

"It is a little thin, and often tangled here, for I have no comb, but when it is smooth it looks very well."

"Yes?"

"My eyes are dark too. My teeth are fine and small and white, though a little crowded in my mouth. My face is very pale, and I am scrawny but very strong. And I have small hands."

"Yes?"

"I have a light step, my mistress said of me."

"I think of you as having a light step."

"Why?"

"Because so often, I do not hear you move toward me

before you speak, but I hear from your voice that you are very near."

"Because I whisper?" I said, whispering as I said it.

"Yes."

Then we both laughed softly, though neither could have said why.

"Why did you take the gloves?"

This stopped me laughing.

"What is that to you?"

"Because I think of how you must be hanged. And I want to know why."

"To have one thing in the world that was mine," I replied, echoing what I had said to Madame Pommereau. For it was true, and suddenly I wanted to tell him a simple truth about myself, and see how he took it.

"Yes," he said at last. "Yes, that makes sense."

"And yet they will hang me for it."

"It is a shame."

"I think of the gloves sometimes. I wonder if she wears them again now."

"Would she do so?"

"I don't know. Perhaps she keeps them stuffed at the very back of her drawer, so she will not see them. I like to think it is painful to her to see them, because it puts her in mind of me, and that she feels guilt for what she did to me."

"So she should. She should feel guilty forever."

I waited, not speaking. I heard a rising anger in his voice

and was pleased by it.

"I hate women like that," he said, "ladies who cannot lift a finger, or do anything at all. They are not fit for this land. They are useless, such people."

"She was useless, Jean. And pig-ignorant. She couldn't even dress herself. She couldn't even lace her own shoes. She couldn't even make a fist! Useless!"

"Useless!"

"Useless!"

"A useless bitch! They should hang *her*! They should wring her neck like a useless rat!"

The force of his words startled us both, for no one calls such a woman such names, and I think we both glanced over our shoulders, prisoners though we were, as though someone might have heard us.

"Is there no way out?" he said at last.

"Not here," I said, solemn. "I think there is not, here. I must be hanged. It is a shame."

"Tell me something else," he said, and I could hear him shifting on the other side of the wall.

"Tell you what?"

"Anything else."

"There is nothing else for me."

"Well, it is a long time yet."

"Perhaps when you leave here, there will still be no hangman."

"I had not thought of that."

"That you will leave before they hang me?"

"I will be sorry to leave you here," he said. "I had not thought that anything would make me sorry to leave this place."

"I will be sorry too, Jean, with no one left to talk to."

Then we were quiet again.

"Jean?"

"Yes?"

"My mistress told me a tale once. She told me that if a woman is condemned to death by hanging, she can marry the hangman and so be pardoned."

He laughed, a short sharp sound, not meant to be funny.

"Well, that is bad luck for you, for there is no hangman to marry."

"If I could make a man become the hangman and then marry me, I would be saved."

"Better to hang," he said curtly.

"Why?"

"Because it would be a shameful way to live, married to the hangman."

"It would be more shameful to die. All that lives wishes to go on living, Jean. Even the most shameful life might have some honor in it somewhere, but death has no honor at all."

"No. A woman who married the hangman would be shamed always, and her husband shamed worse."

I saw there was nothing to gain by this, not yet.

"Tell me …"

"What?"

"Tell me about the man you killed."

There was a longer silence then.

"Jean?"

"What if …"

"Yes?"

"Can I tell you something, Françoise, and you will not think less of me?"

"Anything at all, anything."

"You must not laugh at me."

"I would never laugh. Come now, I have told you many secrets, and I began by telling you a lie, so even the scales and confess your sins!"

He sighed, but still would not go on.

"Is it very terrible?" I asked.

When he spoke, his voice was so chastened I had to strain to hear it.

"I never killed a man at all, Françoise. It was a duel, but it was nothing, it was so quick. I wounded him in the fingers of his right hand, just a little nick with my sword, and then it was over. They put me in here as a punishment for dueling, but that was all it was—a nick, a nothing."

I did not speak, waiting for him to go on.

"I am only a drummer boy, Françoise. I have never hurt anyone; I had not even handled a sword before that day. The other soldiers called me a child and cuffed me about the head. And so, when it was past enduring, I challenged to a duel the one who had been most insulting to me. He was young, nearly as young as I was, but he was a cruel creature. I thought thus to prove myself a man. Yet all I managed was to break his skin with the sword, and I did not even know how to wield it. I must have looked a great fool. So I was disgraced before they ever sent me to prison. I am not as I have shown myself to you."

There was such misery in his voice that I was moved, and felt almost that I could weep, but I kept my ear to the hole.

"And then I was here in the dark, alone, and I thought: I am a coward. And when I heard you, I thought, I will tell her what I wish was true, and she will not think me a coward. She will think I am fierce and brave. So I lied as well as you did."

I listened, waiting.

"You must think me a terrible liar, now, and not worth speaking to."

"It is only a story, Jean. You only told me a story."

He sniffled.

"And I do not think you a coward. There are other ways of being brave. Other ways you could be valiant. As I am sure you are."

"What ways?"

"Many ways. And I am pleased, too, that you would wish for me to think you such a fearsome soldier."

"Don't laugh."

"I'm not laughing. Or, I do not laugh at you. I laugh because my heart feels light."

"And you do not think I am a coward, truly?"

"No. Let me say something now, Jean."

"What?"

"I lied to you at first, but I will not lie anymore. Let us be truthful with each other. As much as we can. But let us have some stories, all the same."

"Françoise?"

"Yes?"

"Why did you say it was only a story, not a lie? What is the difference?"

"Because stories are how we keep ourselves from going mad, here."

"In these cells?"

"These cells. This land. This world. Jean, let us not be liars too much, but for God's sake, let us tell stories to bear our burdens better! It is all we have!"

"You'll wake the warden, yelling so."

"I'll whisper then. Come closer."

"I can't come any closer, my ear is touching the wall as it is."

"Fair enough. Here's what I will say: I am the last on this earth of all my family, and I am not going to die yet. I was born to escape, or I would not have moved up so high, nor fallen so far. I was born to escape, do you see?"

"No. Escape how? Gnaw through the door with your sharp little teeth?"

"Wait and see, Jean. Wait and see."

I settled back into the straw as we talked, looking up at the roof of my cell and hearing the endless drip of the water along the wet stones. I thought of cowards and heroes and the ways in which young men cannot face shame, and the ways they wish for glory, for a mission to undertake. I would save him from his greatest fear and make him feel himself a hero, a savior, my savior.

I wondered, thinking of Jean, whether I was a creature without honor or scruple. But I did not care. Plans spun in my head until I was dizzy with them, thinking of ways and means, of when and how.

Chapter Twenty

It was all very well to plan and plot in my own mind, but time ran on fast and I found myself beset by fears, unable to put my plans into action.

I had never thought much of being courted. Courting was a word for ladies, not for girls like me who were more likely to muck about with a ruffian in an alley and hope to shame him into marriage later than to be courted as ladies are courted in ballads and books. Though even that, I was not so sure of, thinking of Madame Pommereau traveling a great way over the water, alone, to marry a man she had not met. Perhaps even the courtship of gentlemen and ladies was a matter only for ballads, not for life.

But whether or not this was so, in this case I would need to do the courting myself, and the thought of it baffled me and crippled my speech.

All that week I could not think how to turn the talk toward marriage, or nooses, or hanging, or my own escape. I could not ask him straight out to marry me and save my life. I knew, even knowing him only a little, that he would not accept such a proposal. He would need to make the offer himself, and he must be frightened, or tricked, or led into it. But how was I to lead?

And under that, a sneaking small voice in my head wished for him to come to it himself, and not be led by me. Perhaps, for all my tough and hardened heart (for was I not Françoise Laurent, a vicious character?), I wished also, simply, to be rescued for myself, and not for my trickery. I knew I had to make him ask me, someway, and yet I also wished, against all sense, to be saved without having to ask for it.

But no one ever gets exactly what she wants in this world. And I was thinking like a soft fool. Or like a girl who listens too closely to old songs, whether or not she will admit it.

※ ※ ※

"You are dull," he said one morning, when I had barely spoken for hours. "What is the matter?"

"Nothing is the matter."

"That's not so, or why would you have nothing to say?"

"I am only melancholy, Jean."

"Well, don't be," he said, petulant, "for then I have no one to talk to."

I did not answer.

"I am sorry," he went on at last. "I should remember better what you must face."

I still did not answer.

"But it cannot be helped, is that not so? And if it cannot be helped, it must not be minded, for it does no good. And think of it this way: you at least know the manner of your death. The rest of us must wonder, but you know."

"What is that to me?"

"Well," he said slowly, "perhaps it may bring you rest, this knowing. Or it may be a kind of power, to see the future, don't you think?"

"That is easy for you to believe, safe as you are."

"I know. You do not need to keep reminding me."

Seeing the future. I thought of Marie, Isabelle, their shivering scared milky faces, the candles and the mirror, the imagined woman. *I can see the future, so I know.*

"Fate," I said aloud.

"What?"

"You say I have power because I know my fate."

"I suppose that is what I mean."

"What if I knew your fate as well?"

"But you don't."

Then the warden came, rattling keys.

"Bread," he said, opening my door, "and naught else, I'm afraid."

He looked at me with less friendliness than before.

"Do not waste so much time whispering through walls."

"What is that to you?"

"Do not be so sharp. Thinking too much of earthly things, like soldiers in their coats, and not on your final judgment." His face was sour, but his eyes, I saw, were kindly still. I knew he had felt fatherly toward me, and was in a fatherly manner disappointed, thinking me shallow or conniving. Looking at him, I felt a great wave of tiredness at the thought of people being disappointed in me. I chafed under it.

"Go on then. Leave my food and go on."

He went on, grumbling, to my neighbor's door.

Then I heard Jean's voice.

"Could I not have a sight of her?"

The warden laughed.

"No. She's much the same as any other girl would be, stuffed in here and scared out of her wits. But I cannot give you the sight of her, I have orders, like everyone else."

Then I heard the door slam. And we both listened to the retreating steps.

"Jean."

"Yes?"

"That was good of you."

"I would like very much to see you," he said formally.

"Maybe you will."

"How? You're a thief, they'll hang you for a thief."

"Do you really wish to see me?"

"Yes."

I gathered my courage.

"When you leave here …"

"What? You are always beginning speeches and not finishing! It is provoking!"

"Will you think often of me?"

"Yes," he said, his voice serious, "I will think often of you."

I pressed my forehead against the stone, spoke again into the hole.

"Jean. There is a way you could see me."

"No!"

I drew back, startled. I had expected at least to get a few more words in.

"Don't spoil it!" he cried at me. "I can't! Ever since you told me, I am always afraid you will say it! I can't!"

"Jean—"

"I have thought of it. But it is a fearful thing. I am too afraid to save you. I am a coward. To knot the rope, to deal out death in that cold way, is too horrible …"

"But to save my life."

"No."

His voice was hard, but the hardness did not fool me. I knew it was to keep out tears.

"I have thought of it, Françoise. I have thought often of it, these past days and nights. I have wished, even, that I were not afraid. But it is too much to ask of me. I am a coward." I heard him fling away from the wall. I heard him kick over his plate and cup, and kick his boots against the stones, and curse soft, private curses, not against me, but against himself. I knew I had to reassure him now, if I were not to lose the game altogether.

"Jean—"

"No."

"Wait."

"What?"

"Calm yourself. It will be well."

"No. It will never be. They will hang you, and I can't save you."

I could hear him, still kicking about the cell.

"Jean."

I waited. At last, the noise stilled.

"Are you there, Jean?"

"Yes."

"Don't be troubled by what you cannot help. You can't save me, then, no matter how much I want to be saved. Eat, drink."

"I can't eat or drink, for I've kicked over all the dishes."

"The more fool you, my lad. Go to sleep hungry then, but do not fear."

He laughed at my teasing tone, and though it was a shaky, unsteady laugh, I joined in, just to encourage him.

"Françoise—"

"Go to sleep. When you wake up, I'll be here."

I smiled as I said it, and he heard the smile in my voice.

When he was quiet, I stayed by the hole, leaning against the wall. The summer season had passed and the air felt chill. Soon, I thought, they will let him go. The leaves will fall from all the trees, unseen by me, and then it will be very cold. I will lie here in the cold dark, alone forever. When winter comes, will it be so cold that I will freeze to death on these stones before they ever find a hangman to put the noose round my neck?

He cried out then, perhaps from a nightmare. He was very young, in that cry.

I put my mouth to the hole, blew soft into it, hoping to catch him on the very edge of his sleep.

"Jean."

No answer.

That was all to the good. I did not want an answer, yet. I wanted only to somehow enter that sleep, to find the chink and force myself in. *I can tell the future, so I know.*

"Jean."

He stirred, but still did not answer.

"Oh, the pleasure of love is fleeting. But the sorrow of love lasts." I sang this low, coaxing, and I waited.

"Do you know how I know that song?" I asked.

"No," he said, his voice faint, bleared, not yet fully awake.

"I know it from you. You used to sing it in the market. And I know the shape of the scar on your hand, Jean, and I know the precise red of your hair. I know the way the sun shone on the first day you were ever a recruit, and how you feared to muddy your boots. I could tell you the expression on your face that day. No, don't ask me questions. Just listen. Listen to me. And when I am finished, you will see your fate. I can see the future, so I know. Just listen."

I shifted, keeping my voice quiet and slow. I was a hunter now, and above all, I must be soft, and patient.

"Forget the nightmare you had, forget what made you cry out just now. I know what it was about, one way or another. It was a dream of fear, yes? All nightmares come from the same fear, of the same thing. But I can show you a way out, Jean. I can show you your fear, and show you that you need never be afraid again."

He was more wakeful now. I could hear him shifting toward the hole.

I made myself be silent. I waited to hear his breath. I waited till he could hear mine, and then, slowly, I moved my breath in time with his own.

"Jean. Most in the world, you wish not to be a coward, yes?"

He shifted his weight, flinching.

"Saving me, you would never be afraid again. You would be free of cowardice forever."

Still he listened; still I made myself speak low.

"And what do you fear most, Jean? What is at the heart of your fear? Death. Call it one thing or another, but you fear death. That is what we all fear. And so you fear to have conference with death, to deal in death, because it makes it so near. But what if I showed you that you could triumph over death by being so near to it? More than any soldier does."

I dropped my voice even lower, so he had to lean in very close to listen.

"You have never killed a man. A soldier, and never killed a man! It is a shame! But as the hangman, you would kill many. And you would not be some soldier, swinging blindly, hoping for luck and an easy kill. You would be Death—slow, deliberate, and inescapable as Death himself. It is a fearful thing, to be Death to so many. You would not only deal in death, you would be Death's representative. And that is why people revile the hangman, that is why he is despised, that is why no one is willing to be a hangman in all of New France.

Because their despising is really fear of the task. They are all cowards. But I know that the task is liberation, not disgrace. It is bravery to undertake it, for someone must. Someone must say 'yes, I will' and that someone must be a man who has put aside all doubt, all fear. If you became the hangman, you would be no coward. Because you would be Death: the most fearful thing there was. And so you would have no need to fear. I know that because I am looking at Death every day, and Death will be my husband, unless you, being my husband instead, will take Death's place. You are afraid of what I say. It makes sense to be afraid; you would be a fool if you had no fear. But listen to me: go beyond your fear and you will conquer it. The most dreadful thing you could imagine would be your own face in the mirror, and who could ever be afraid of that? Ordinary men will say they despise you, but they will not know the truth: you are braver than any of them, and their contempt is only terror masked.

"And you would save me, Jean. I know you. I know exactly where on your chest the top of my head comes to. When you see me, you will see I am no witch. I know these things because I am your fate. And I would know you under the mask of Death that you would wear, I would know you exactly as you were: the bravest of them all. I would be the truest and the strongest you would ever find. I would see beyond anything the world saw, and see the power you held in yourself. Think of it! You would be the most frightful thing you could ever know! And I would know it, and honor you for it. Because you would have saved me.

"And we would make a life thus. Shall I tell you about this life?"

"Yes," he said, whispering also.

"If you leave here without me, what will that be? A few years of soldiering, of boredom, of cards and drink, the dreary sameness of each day. I know that life. It is the life my father lived. And you are destined for greater things than that. For where does that life lead? Death in battle, not even a noble battle but some skirmish somewhere that no one will remember in ten years' time. Not even in your own fight, with honor. You would just be a scared drummer boy, cut down by some rampaging Englishman or trampled under a maddened horse. Or wounded, going through life limping, waiting for a pension that never comes. And that is not the worst thing. There is something worse besides. If you leave here without me, you will have killed me, Jean. And you will never forget it. I will haunt you. Not as a ghost, but as a memory. The memory of what you might have had instead, the memory of me, and the bloodguilt on your hands. You could have saved me, but you failed. And that is real cowardice. That will make your life a burden to you. I do not threaten. I simply tell the truth.

"But I can save you from that, being your wife. I would be grateful, Jean. I would owe you everything, I would owe you myself, and I would never forget that, not for a moment.

I would make you a home, a place to rest, a place to come back to. I would see your courage, and I would honor you always; with every breath I would remember what you had done for me. You would be luckier than any other husband on earth, Jean. What do they get from their wives? A little love, for a while, and then indifference, or maybe even anger, disappointment? That is all you could expect. But from me, you would get pure and perfect gratitude. And love, which is the same thing. I promise."

I had meant to go on, but my voice caught in my throat. Because, speaking all this, telling the best story I had ever told, I realized it was true. Whether speaking it made it true (for that is the strangeness of words) or whether speaking it made me know it to be true, I could not tell. But in that moment, I found I loved him. He was all I had left to love, and the force of it knocked the wind out of me so that I could not speak. I had been desperate before, but suddenly I was doubly so, afraid to lose myself, but also to lose him, and knowing these things would happen at the same time.

The silence between us was heavy for a space. I did not know what to say, or what he wished me to say, and so said only what I felt.

"Jean?"

"Yes."

"I'm here."

"Yes."

"I will always be."

For a moment, I thought he was about to speak.

"Don't say anything. Just think of all I've said."

He did not answer me. And then I heard him turn away.

Chapter Twenty-one

All the next day, he said nothing.

I huddled on the far side of the wall, eyeing the crack. I willed a sound to come from it, any sound at all. But I did not ask, did not speak his name, did not come any nearer.

The light from my little window crawled across the floor. I watched it.

The warden came with the morning meal.

"Well, my girl, I've some hard news," he said, keeping his eyes away from mine and staring at a spot above my head.

I waited.

"A man came forward yesterday and said he was willing to be the hangman. Most likely they will take him on, and a date will be set for you. And I fear it will be soon."

From the other side of the wall I heard the sharp sound of Jean's breath.

"If it is any comfort, he is a great burly fellow, and will tie a sound knot."

He came and patted my shoulder awkwardly, as if he did not know what else to do.

"I've not done this in all my days, but I've never seen a girl as young as you hanged. I will ask him, as a favor, to look the other way and let you jump, so that you may snap your own neck. Clean and quick. You won't feel it."

Then he set down my cup and plate and left me.

I could not eat. I heard him give Jean his ration, but Jean made no sound when the warden asked him how he did.

I turned away from the hole and hid my face in my knees.

As the minutes crawled by in silence, I considered myself. I had failed. Jean had not said a word, and they had found a man to hang me. As for Jean, his time would be served, and they would let him go. And then they would take me before a cheering, jeering crowd and hang me from a wooden scaffold. Down by the water, where the ships come. I would look out at the water one last time, and gulp down the cold air, and then I would be gone.

And somewhere, lost in the crowd, unknown to me, perhaps he would stand, watching. Would he recognize me, and remember me? Would he feel guilt, sorrow, or simply relief? I would never know.

I twisted the hem of my gray smock into my mouth, for I felt a great cry of despair trying to get out of me. I had missed my one chance, and now it was too late.

The light faded from the window. I sat still as a stone.

The warden came and brought my supper. Seeing I had eaten nothing, he asked me if I was ill.

I did not answer. Sighing, he scooped up my breakfast and left the dinner portion, and went out.

I heard him go into Jean's cell. I stuffed my fingers in my ears, not wanting to hear Jean's voice.

Perhaps Jean would never speak to me again now. From

shame, from fear, or simply from the wish to be rid of me.

I curled myself up in my corner, fanning my skirt around me. I pretended I lay within a charmed circle, protected.

It was wholly dark now. Outside I heard wind in the branches of the few spindling trees that grew by these walls, and a low, soft sound, like an owl calling.

The moon rose, a blind white disk above me. Still I lay within the circle.

Then, at last, I heard movement from the other side of the wall, and then, a voice.

"Françoise? Françoise?"

Falling over my skirts, I hurtled toward the hole. In the dark, I cracked my head on the stones.

"Yes?"

I held my head, tears starting in my eyes.

"Françoise. Are you there?"

"I'm here. I'm here."

When he spoke again, his voice sounded cracked and dry.

"Will you marry me?"

"Yes. I will. Yes."

Chapter Twenty-two

The rest of that night we lay side by side, the wall between us. We calculated as best we could where his hand was, where mine, and touched our fingertips together, with the stones between. I had no words left after my speech of the night before, and he also had nothing to say. So there we were, nervous, strangers, trying to be glad and yet afraid as well. For he was not yet the hangman, and I was not yet free, and neither of us knew how all this was to be accomplished. Considering this, I thought I would never sleep, and yet I must have, for I woke in the morning cold and stiff.

I had shifted in my sleep and found I lay curled, my hands under my chin. The hole out of which his question had come seemed small and insignificant in the morning light.

"Françoise?"

"Yes."

"Did you sleep?"

"Did you?"

"I must have, for I dreamed."

His voice sounded hesitant.

"Jean?"

"What?"

"Nothing, nothing."

Silence for a stretch.

"Françoise?"

"What?"

"No, nothing."

I gripped my fingers together, nerved myself to speak plain.

"Jean?"

"What?"

"Have you changed your mind?"

"If you spoke to me truly, then I have not."

"I did, Jean. I meant all I said."

"Then so did I."

I sighed with relief, and he echoed it, which made me grin.

"We're a fine pair, Jean."

"How?"

"If we cannot even speak frankly, it will be hard to accomplish marriage. Here we are, hemming and hawing like geese, and both too shy to say what we mean."

"I suppose we will learn."

"You will learn, you mean. I think wives are meant to be silent and say nothing. Or only speak when spoken to, is that not so?"

"I don't know. I have no experience."

"Well, if it is so, you will be saddled with a poor excuse for a wife, for I never stop talking, and I must have the last word in everything."

We both laughed then. I did not know who began it, or if anything was truly funny, but we couldn't stop. We chortled and shook and tears came into our eyes, we laughed so hard.

"What a trick!" Jean shouted, at the height of it. "What a trick we've played!"

"What a joke!"

"The warden, the judge, all the officers and the rest, all expecting me to crawl out of here and back to the army shamed and sorry, and the Pommereaus waiting to see you hang dead on the scaffold! But we've cheated them all!"

"They'll be so surprised, they'll all piss themselves when they hear!"

"And your old mistress, she'll die of shock! She'll never believe it!"

"And we'll dance on their graves, Jean! On everyone's grave!"

"No one can touch us!"

"Not us! We'll surprise anyone who thinks they know the end of this story!"

We subsided, giggling like foolish children.

"What do we do now, Françoise?" he asked, more serious.

"What next, do you mean?"

"How am I to become the hangman if they have a man already, and get them to let you out, and then …"

"And marry me?"

"And marry you."

We both laughed again, but less sure this time. Saying it baldly, in the daylight, it seemed harder to think on seriously than when I whispered promises to him in the darkness. Better to laugh at it. But now I must think of ways and means. I could see I would have to lead him, in this.

"Well, Jean. We must ask the warden, then. He will know."

I spoke confidently, but underneath I felt a small doubt. Not of myself, for any doubts I had were worthless: I had no other choice worth having. But for Jean. I felt a heaviness gathered in my stomach, remembering he must not falter. He had much to do now, and my salvation rested entirely on his resolve. What if the terror of what he was promising hit him all at once, and he found it was too much to promise?

"Warden!"

I heard him jump up as he called through the bars of his cell.

"What are you doing?"

"No time like the present," he said, his voice sure. "We shall seize the day, Françoise. Warden!"

"Shall we not first consider—"

"No. We have no time to lose. We shall embark on action! I shall be a man of action now. As you say, I must have no fear. Warden!"

I joined in the shouting now, and our yells rang down the corridor.

"Warden!"

"WARDEN!"

"WARDEN!"

We heard a door opening, steps, muttering. We kept

yelling. All our wildness returned, as when we had laughed, but we were serious now. As the warden approached, we called out together, and I realized, suddenly, that we would be together now, for good or ill. I was not only being given my life back, I was beginning a new one. With this thought, I fell silent while Jean kept calling until the warden stopped at his door, wheezing with anger.

"WARDEN! WARDEN!"

"God's blood, I'm right in front of you, damn you! Can you not see? Can you not hear? For your own sakes, I hope there is a fire, or a flood, or one of you has killed the other through that hole you like to whisper through, for if it's anything less I'll have you whipped."

"Warden, let me out."

"Have you lost your senses?"

"No, but you must let me out."

"Enough foolishness. You waste my time. Good-bye."

"Wait!"

"If you keep raving, I will flay you both myself. You shall not have an inch of unbroken skin on your backs."

I heard him moving away from the door, then Jean's voice, high and excited.

"Warden, let me out. I'm going to marry her."

In the silence that followed I imagined the warden's face, his jaw hanging slack with shock. When Jean spoke again I heard the glee in his voice.

"Tell me what I must do, for I'm to marry her."

"You marry a dead girl, sir. She shall hang, and she shall hang soon."

"No she shall not, Warden. For I will become the hangman, and then marry her, and so we shall both be free. Come, I am determined. You must instruct me in what I must now do to achieve all this, for I've made my choice."

I heard the warden stepping back toward us, followed by the clanking of Jean's cell door. Quickly, I put my ear to the hole, straining to hear what was said.

" ... consider, sir, your immortal soul. Them that put nooses on necks shall answer for it at the last judgment—"

"We all shall answer!" I cried through the hole. "And a hangman only carries out the judgment of man, same as a soldier does. Or a prison warden! How are you any better?"

He went on to Jean as if I had not spoken.

"Consider also, sir, your youth and inexperience. You do not know what it is you do, my boy. You walk into a trap. I am sorry to say it, for she's a good enough girl and it is a great shame she is to be hanged. But all the same, let me speak to you as an older and wiser man, who has seen much. It is a bad life, the life of a hangman. Let another man do it. Perhaps she has bewitched you with pretty ways and clever speeches, but do not let yourself be led blindly. Wait out your sentence. Win your freedom. You will find you forget her."

Then Jean spoke.

"I have given my word. Tell me what I am to do."

"And if I refuse to help you, for your own good—"

"Then you have no shame, Warden, and meddle in what you do not understand. I have given my word, and I will not be made faithless for my own good."

The warden sighed, and his voice was grieved.

"Well, sir, your word is sacred. Keep it. I will aid you as I can, though it is against my better judgment. But good luck to you. You'll need it."

I heard him leave the cell, and come to mine. He did not open my door, but hissed at me through it.

"As for you, lass. You've had great luck, or you're the devil himself, or both. You've ensnared him, for certain, and he's only a boy. I thought it was a wicked thing to hang you, and so it is, but you've dragged a young creature down into the mud with you, and you're no better than a whore now."

It did not hurt me. If I could have my freedom, anyone might call me anything they liked. But Jean breathed sharply.

"Do not speak to her so."

Then an astonishing thing happened.

"I am sorry, sir," the warden said. "If your mind is made up, then I will not call your bride such things."

He stepped quickly backward away from my cell and back along the corridor.

Jean laughed.

"I put him in his place."

He said it almost to himself. I wished to say that I could have done the same, that he had no need to speak for me. Then I realized that it pleased him, to speak for me. And that the warden also had begged pardon because now I, to him, belonged to Jean, and so they spoke of me as man to man, and their exchange had little to do with me. So I was silent, wondering what it was, indeed, that I had promised him, in promising myself.

Then the warden returned.

"Now, tell me what I must do," said Jean briskly. I could hear pride and a new resolution in his voice. I had told Jean that he would be brave, and hearing him, I knew he found himself brave, and that this surprised and pleased him.

"Well, sir, I have never had such a case before, not in all my days here, but I know the form the law must follow. We all have heard of this law, but I never thought to see it enacted."

"Let it be something to tell your grandchildren, then, and get on with it."

"You must make a petition in writing. You must first ask to be released from your imprisonment, and swear that in return, you will perform the duties of hangman for all of New France. And you must take this petition before the authorities and use all your powers of persuasion to convince them that you are the best man to be hangman. Do that however you may. Rant and rave of your love for the girl, to see if that plays on their heartstrings, or say your father was a rope maker. I care not. Then, if you are accepted, you must make a second formal petition, asking for the release of this girl, and swearing that you will make her your wife."

"And then …"

"And then, if they accept these petitions, she will be released, and you will be married, and God help you."

"Give me the paper and tell me what I must say."

I heard the rustle of paper, and a quill scratching.

"Let me see her now."

I held my breath.

"No. Until she's free and you're free, I am still bound by law. Now, repeat after me."

❊ ❊ ❊

"Jean. Is he gone?"

"Yes."

"Pass me what it is you wrote."

"I will read it aloud."

"No, please. I heard much of it already, but I wish to see it. See if it will go through the hole, rolled tight."

"Why?"

"I must see it, Jean. It will seem real when I see it."

I heard the crinkling dry sound of folding paper.

Then, two pieces of paper were pushed, scraping, through that small chink.

I spread them out on my lap, carefully avoiding any damp or dirt, and read.

I, JEAN COROLÈRE, do humbly Petition to be

Released from my term of Imprisonment, and in Exchange to Serve as HANGMAN for all New France, in the Year of our LORD 1751. I will faithfully undertake all the duties proper to this Office for as long as I live. May God have Mercy upon my Soul.

And then the second, which seemed more looping, as if written in greater haste.

I, JEAN COROLÈRE, having petitioned to be Released from my Imprisonment to Serve as HANGMAN, do request and entreat that upon my Release there be the Release also of the Person named FRANÇOISE LAURENT, who is Condemned to Die by Hanging. And I hereby, before God, announce my intention to Marry the said FRANÇOISE LAURENT, thereby absolving her of her Crimes and giving her over to my Care for as long as we both shall Live. May God have Mercy upon my Soul.

I smoothed the papers with shaking hands.

"Françoise?"

"What?"

"Do you weep?"

"No."

"Liar." There was laughter in his voice, but kindness too.

"Only a little." I wiped my eyes.

I rolled the papers up, slid them carefully back through the wall.

"Why do you weep?"

"Because it seems you mean it, after all."

"I would not say it if I did not mean it. It is a serious thing."

I saw he did not know what I meant: to say a thing and mean it, and then to find you do not mean it, later. To make something true by speaking it, and then find it less certain as soon as it is no longer spoken aloud. Perhaps he was simpler than I. Perhaps I did not mind that.

"Tell me what you will do now."

I knew well enough—I'd been listening to everything he and the warden had said—but I wanted to hear him say it, and I knew he wanted to tell.

"Tomorrow, Françoise, he will come for me. He will bring me my uniform. I will put it on, and wear my soldier's boots, and I will make myself smart. I will put the letters in my pocket. And I will go before the authorities and make my case. And I shall be brave, Françoise. I will not falter in the task, I will plead my case well. I shall make you proud of me forever. And they will be persuaded, and accept my petition, and tell the other man to go his own way. I know. You have given me courage, and I will win the day. You'll see."

We were both crouched at the hole now, and his voice lowered.

"And the next day, Françoise, the next day I will make another petition. For you. And they will come and let you out."

"And you will be waiting for me."

"Yes."

"And you will see me."

"Yes."

"Jean?"

"What?"

"Nothing."

❀ ❀ ❀

The next day, he left. I heard him dressing himself in his uniform, lacing his boots, I heard him click his heels, as if to practice. He sang softly as he made ready.

All that time he said no word to me. I hovered, listening. I wanted to speak to him, but did not know what I should say. I crossed my fingers, hoping my luck would hold.

Then the warden came. I heard Jean's door swing open, hitting against the wall. Jean's boots rang out against the stones.

"Are you ready?" he asked Jean.

"Yes."

Then, turning, Jean called to me.

"Françoise. Tomorrow I will see you."

"Now then," said the warden, "come along."

I heard steps, loud and sure, then fading, then gone. Faintly, a door slammed far away down the passage.

I was left alone.

Chapter Twenty-three

The day and night passed somehow, in pacing and uneasy sleep. And the next day I smoothed my skirts, wiped my face as best I could, combed my hair with my fingers, and stood, waiting for the door to open.

I looked about the cell. I had served my time here, as long as I had served my lady. I stood in the very center of it, in the square of dust-filled light from the window, a strong, keen light, for it was now midday.

I had thought these walls would be my tomb. I had lain on the floor, unable to lift my head, my clothes seeped through with damp, waiting for death. And now I must fix all my thoughts upon Jean, his newfound bravery, his will. If he could be bold, quick, persuasive as I knew myself to be, then they would let me out. I would leave here forever, and not with a rope about my neck.

And then what?

I pushed away that thought. It was too big, too uncertain. And it was now too late to ponder it. I was in the grip of my strange fate, and would see it through. I would marry the hangman.

Something glittering in the corner caught my eye. Stooping, I gathered up the fragments of my broken mirror.

It was mostly shards, silver slivers too little for any use, but there were one or two larger pieces. Careful of my fingers, I found the bent and twisted frame and laid the shards of mirror inside it, seeing the oval of glass take shape. There were gaps and cracks, but there it was.

Peering into it, I was surprised, almost, to see I had exactly the same face. I thought perhaps that all my trials and desperate ventures would have marked me more. But I was still a thin, spindling, pale thing, with dark hair hanging loose, quick eyes, a small determined mouth. I was a little older, and I looked tired, but I was the same girl who had stood looking into Madame Pommereau's mirror. Even in my prison smock, I was still myself, as I had been in my borrowed finery and the rags of my parents' home.

The sight of my face troubled me, for the missing slivers gave the effect of holes, as if I were unstable, shifting, unreal. I thought of my future life. My reflection put me in mind of conjuring the woman in the mirror: Show me a husband. Now I would see him plain. The red-haired, fierce, dreaming boy who'd chased me through the streets; the young recruit, arrogant and full of watchful fear, wishing for great things, terrified of shame. And now the hangman, whatever that would mean.

Whatever I had whispered in the dark, I knew we would both shrink from the knowledge of what it was he did, what necks he broke, what tears or prayers he heard. I would make a haven for him, a place to forget the lives he took. I understood that I must do that now and forever. I must give him a place to make up for what I had asked him to become. What he had become, for me. I must make it up to him, in gratitude for my salvation. It felt, in that moment, a burden too great to bear.

I shivered. What would we say when we saw each other for the first time? In the light, no walls, what would we find to say? Would he remember me? Would I disappoint him? Would we love each other, as I had promised?

I strained to hear the key turning in the lock, opening the door of my cell. But all was still. What if he had failed in the task, seeming only a timid boy unhardened to the world? What if they had laughed at his petition, and mocked him for being taken in by me, called me a whore as the warden had done? Indeed, what if Jean had changed his mind, and would not come for me? Seeing the air, the day, the bustle of the town, all the richness of life outside these walls, perhaps he would discover that I had asked for what he could not give. It is easy to feel the magic of a stranger in such a dreary place, but with the whole world open before him, I might fade.

I looked again into the mirror. I saw the set of my chin, the life of my eyes. I would not fade. I would triumph. Jean would neither fail nor forget me. I had won, against all odds, against death, against the fate others had set before me. Anyone who liked might call me shameful, but I would not feel shame.

I would be free. And I would carry with me my escape,

and whatever waited beyond these walls, that knowledge would give me strength. I nodded to my reflection. And then I smiled.

Behind me, I heard the door open. I gathered up the pieces of my mirror and hid them in my pocket, wrapped in a handkerchief.

"Françoise. Come out."

And I turned and walked through the low doorway to where he stood, waiting for me.

※

Historical Note

The basic facts of this story are true. Françoise Laurent, daughter of a Montreal soldier, was a servant in the Pommereau household. In 1751, she was convicted of stealing from Madame Pommereau and sentenced to hang. Other than letters of annulment, remission, or pardon, the only way a woman could escape such a sentence was to marry the hangman. But at the time of Françoise's sentence, the hangman, Jean-Baptiste Duclos, had recently died. Waiting for a replacement to be found, she discovered that her neighbor was a young soldier named Jean Corolère, who was serving a light sentence as a punishment for dueling, having wounded a soldier called Coffre in one finger of his right hand. According to the *Dictionary of Canadian Biography*, "the young criminal decided therefore to ensnare Corolère so completely that he would be ready to do anything to marry her, even serve as hangman, a role considered dishonorable at the period. After some months as his neighbor she had achieved her ends." How she did this, no one knows. In August of 1751, Jean Corolère petitioned to be released from his sentence in order to serve as hangman, and was accepted. He presented a second petition the following day, begging the authorities to "grant him in marriage the person named Françoise Laurent."

I have concocted Françoise's story around these bare facts. All other details about her are imagined.

Corolère certainly served as hangman. However, after 1752, "all trace of him and his wife is lost."

Acknowledgments

The Hangman in the Mirror has a parallel life as a play based on the same set of historical facts. The play, *The Hanging of Françoise Laurent*, was co-created by performers Sarah Cormier, Zach Fraser, Kiersten Tough, and me (as writer-director). Huge thanks to Sarah, Zach, and Kiersten for their brilliance, verve, and generosity, and for allowing me to run with the story in another form.

Thanks to Katie Hearn for a thoughtful, patient, and rigorous editorial eye, for guiding the story in the right direction, and for graciously dealing with my second guessing along the way. Thanks to everyone at Annick for all their work.

Thanks to the Ontario Arts Council for supporting me at points during the writing of the book, and to the publishers who recommended me for funding through the OAC's Writers' Reserve Program.

Thanks to the librarians at the Toronto Reference Library, for helping me to find images that inspired sections of the story.

Thanks to Rachael Cayley, Mia Feldbruegge, and Jane Price for reading early drafts of the manuscript. And thanks to Lea Ambros, for everything.